PERFECTION
IN BAD AXE

PERFECTION
IN BAD AXE

STORIES BY CRAIG BERNTHAL

University of Missouri Press
Columbia and London

University of Missouri Press, Columbia, Missouri 65201
Printed and bound in the United States of America
All rights reserved
5 4 3 2 1   07 06 05 04 03

Library of Congress Cataloging-in-Publication Data
Bernthal, Craig, 1952–
   Perfection in Bad Axe : stories / by Craig Bernthal.
      p. cm.
   ISBN 0-8262-1481-9 (alk. paper)
   I. Title.
   PS3602.E763P47 2003
   813′.6—dc21
                                                    2003007990

♾™ This paper meets the requirements of the
American National Standard for Permanence of Paper
for Printed Library Materials, Z39.48, 1984.

Designer: Lisa Sanders
Typesetter: The Composing Room of Michigan, Inc.
Printer and binder: The Maple-Vail Book Manufacturing Group
Typefaces: Palatino, Trajan, Vintage Typewriter, Woodtype Ornaments 2

   Six stories originally appeared, in somewhat different form, in the fol-
lowing journals: "A Small Parenthesis in Eternity," *Zyzzyva;* "Route 18,"
Fiction; "A Knight Pursued," *The Apalachee Review;* "Little Round Top,"
Passages North; "Center of Gravity," *Licking River Review;* "Perfection in
Bad Axe," *Talking River Review.*

＋＋　 ≖◈≖　 ＋＋

*Publication of this book has been assisted
by the William Peden Memorial Fund.*

To Gail, Sarah, and Luke

I am deeply grateful to my teachers, Steve Yarbrough,
David Borofka, and Liza Wieland.

CONTENTS

PERFECTION IN BAD AXE

A Small Parenthesis
in Eternity

When school ended, I went canoeing for three weeks in the Boundary Waters of Minnesota and Canada. I threw my Timex away, into the first lake, and imagined it ticking all the way to the bottom, where eventually it would stop, be buried, and enter the realm of geologic time, unsegmented and impalpable. If I could free myself from clocks for a whole year, I thought, maybe I could touch the hem of time's garment, maybe then I'd finally understand my place in the world and everyone else's.

I came home twenty pounds lighter. I rested a few weeks and then went back to school for four weeks of field geology. Bill Lindt and I and two other guys decided to travel together in Bill's loose-jointed Ford Falcon. We worked with Brunton compasses in hand, hammers slung in our belts, magnifying lenses hung about our necks with bootlaces. We all slept in Carl's big canvas tent and split food and gas expenses.

The first week, we bombed around the western Upper Peninsula like tourists, not mapping yet, but going from one road cut or mine to the next, stopping to make drawings and hear lectures from Dr. Nordeng.

When we were studying a quarry near Marquette, Bill found the cast-off top of a grill, and part of our cooking problems were solved. The next day we found some wire to hold the sagging gas

1

tank of the Falcon in place. I expected one day we'd hit a bump and detonate. We had a fine campsite on Lake Superior and lived off beer and beans.

Julie Geyer was the only woman in class. She was friendly in a distant way, although she was clearly the odd person out, like an old checker mixed in with a new set. Bill and I had worked together as partners since our first projects as freshmen, and we made a good, tight team, our individual strengths balancing our weaknesses. We'd planned for a year to do the field course together, but I thought, wouldn't it be something to spend the rest of the summer walking in the shade with Julie.

I was waiting for the day when she'd wear a white T-shirt, but she preferred old flannel shirts, buttoned high, with the sleeves ripped off, plus cargo shorts, blue wool socks and shiny new mountain boots. Her hair was as black as her eyes, and, against the fashion, she cut it very short. I ached for Julie Geyer.

I'd first seen her in paleontology. When Dr. Nordeng put out a trilobite or nautilus for the class to draw, she would slowly run her pencil eraser along her bottom lip. She was always one of the last to start actually drawing, but then her slow, steady hand would move over the paper, and long-dead animals would appear, resurrected.

I tried to find out about her from some of the other geology majors, people who were in the class she had started with, but no one had much to say. She'd taken off the year she should have been a sophomore and stayed at home, somewhere downstate, for reasons unknown. She didn't share her apartment with a roommate, and she didn't date much, far as anyone knew, so at least in that sense, she was free. Bill thought she had an attitude; I thought she was filled with sadness, a sorrow so deep it went to the very base of her.

One morning during the second week, Nordeng took us to a site near Michigame, where we were going to make our first map. As usual, Julie had ridden with Nordeng, and standing beside him, she looked like a sapling next to a boulder. "Julie needs to map with somebody, so we'll have to form a group of three . . ."

Nordeng was saying, and before he could finish, I said, "Julie can map with Bill and me. If she wants to." I looked at her and shrugged: "We need all the help we can get." She looked back dubiously. Bill glared at me, tight-lipped, and scuffed the ground with his army surplus 'Nam boots.

Julie tested one of her now-you-see-it-now-you-don't smiles on me. No one else was extending an invitation. "OK," she said to Nordeng.

The area we were assigned to map covered about a hundred acres of relatively old-growth forest with lots of white pine and oak and loose rock. Once the three of us entered the woods, we lost sight of everyone else. Although we couldn't see more than twenty yards in any direction, the forest floor was clear enough to allow comfortable walking.

As usual, we were looking for outcrops, points at which the layers of rock under us broke the surface. Once we found one, we identified the kind of rock that composed it and measured its "strike and dip," the direction of the outcrop where it broke through the earth's surface and the angle of the outcrop as it dipped back into the earth, the dip always being perpendicular to the strike. Our object was practical: find all the outcrops and create a map from which we could extrapolate the position of the iron-bearing strata below.

Integrating Julie into what had become a hermetic partnership was awkward. I took the lead in orienteering. I'd always had a good sense of direction and an accurate pace. My job was to keep track of our position, and I held, on a clipboard, the blank piece of paper that I would eventually fill in to make the map. I was better with a pencil than Bill, who was the locator and identifier of outcrops. He ranged around in front of me like a hunting dog sniffing for pheasant, and he yipped whenever he found bedrock. He measured strikes and dips, and, although I examined the outcrops too, I deferred to him in classification, whether it was shale, slate, or, according to a worn-out joke, just plain schist.

Julie moved softly through the woods, over the cover of pine needles, coming back to me to see how the map was proceeding, going up with Bill to look for outcrops, very serious, very quiet. We were trying to track some slate and iron formations, but the area was packed with glacial drift—rocks and boulders, some the size of small houses, pushed in by glaciers. Big hunks of rock had busted away from the formation we were mapping, which made outcrops hard to distinguish from buried detritus.

I asked Julie if she wanted to do the compass work or draw out the map, but she declined. I struggled to keep my concentration, keep my eyes on target, check the compass, and count paces while being so close to her. As she crouched next to Bill looking at slate, I gazed at the way her hair curled at the nape of her neck, at the delicate wisps and moist ringlets that clung to her skin. I lost myself in the curve of her back when she stooped to examine an outcrop.

Close to noon, I noticed something was wrong. I have a good memory for terrain, and I recognized a boulder with a stunted tree on top that we had come across an hour before, on ground we'd already mapped. We should have been at least fifty yards away from it.

"Oh shit," I muttered.

Julie looked at me quizzically.

"What?" Bill asked.

"I screwed up."

"Why? What's wrong?" he said.

"We've been over this area before."

"How can that be? We've been walking the usual grid." Bill rolled his eyes at me: *Julie,* he was saying.

"OK, let's walk back to the road and watch the compass," I said. Julie looked from me to Bill. We started to walk back, and as we passed close by a big slab of black and rusty rock, maybe eight feet high and thirty feet long, in the space of a dozen paces I watched the compass needle bend toward the rock; by the time I got to the other side of the slab, the needle had been jerked around nearly ninety degrees.

"Look at this," I said. I ran the compass back and forth across the face of the rock.

"Gotta be magnetite," Bill said. He whacked at the rock with his hammer. It was very tough, *competent* is the word, and Bill did a lot of whacking before he could break off a chunk. When he did, he peered at it through his magnifying lens. Then he handed it to me. The clean surface was full of long, black crystals. We moved away from the slab. I ran the chunk over the face of the compass, and the needle followed it like a puppy dog.

We spent the next ten minutes walking around the area, watching the compass needle tack one way and then another as we walked toward the most distant objects we could see. Now that we knew what to look for, we found magnetite all over the place. Sometimes the compass needle veered a little and sometimes a lot, but the anomalies were hard to catch unless you kept your eye on the compass constantly, which would be unnatural, even when mapping.

"We've been walking around in a field of magnetite," Bill said.

I shook my head: "There's not a line on this map that's right."

"Now what?"

"We go in for lunch and confess. We don't have time for anything else." I wrote in capital letters over the top of the map: MAGNETITE, and we trooped in to find Nordeng.

Not far from where we'd parked the cars, Nordeng sat, resting against a white pine. He looked like a human landslide. A picnic hamper was on one side of him, and he had a big red-and-white–checked napkin over his lap. He was nibbling on a cold chicken breast and washing it down with a Miller High Life. When he saw us coming, he delicately blotted his lips with the napkin, a little disappointed at the early disturbance of lunch.

I showed him the map.

He laughed in his throat, and for a while, I wondered whether he was trying to cough up a chicken bone. "How much of this map do you think holds up?" he asked.

"Not much. All we know is, we've got an iron formation over there mixed in with some slate and schist. The lines are totally screwed up."

As the other teams came in, Nordeng eyed their maps stoically.

We were either the only team to figure out we'd been walking in a magnetic maze or the only one to admit it. Whatever, Bill, Julie, and I got the only A's that morning.

Julie had her own pup tent, sleeping bag, and backpack, which she deposited in the Ford Falcon when I invited her to camp with us. I amazed myself. Now that the context of work had been provided, I could talk to her like one of the guys, which at least was a step in the right direction.

With her precise and delicate hand, she became the artist of our threesome. I handled the compass and tried to force my brain beneath the surface of the earth and into the far past. Bill continued as taxonomist and prospector. We didn't rest in our specialties: we all argued about the accuracy of my speculations, Bill's classifications, and even Julie's mapping. Sometimes Julie's smiles lingered.

We hadn't done much heavy walking, but that changed. We mapped larger, more complex areas. We took long hikes up streams, since they, like roadcuts, exposed rock. I noticed one morning, as we made our way around a short waterfall, that Julie was limping.

"Blister?" I asked.

"No."

"Those new boots," I speculated.

"I'm fine."

She sketched at noon. She kept a big artist's pad in her backpack, and after eating a peanut butter and jelly sandwich, she took it out. I'd seen the drawings in her field notebook. Her sketches of rock faces came out in 3-D, and all the shadows and angles made sense. My method of drawing was to focus on all of the details that seemed conceptually important and then to combine them into an indecipherable mass. She began with the whole. I didn't know what she sketching, and she made no effort to show me or anyone else. She concentrated herself within the near space around her and repelled attention.

She limped more as the day went on.

"I've got some blister stuff back in the car," I said.

She just nodded and smiled.

The next morning, while we were taking down the big tent, Julie hobbled out of her pup tent.

"I took care of it," she told me. "All better."

I shook my head.

"Well, you don't have to get exasperated," she said.

"If you took care of it, then why are you still limping around?"

"I put bandages on them."

"I can see it's helping."

She just looked at me.

"Let me do this. It won't take long. Think about how your feet are going to feel by this afternoon."

"How did you become an expert on blisters?" she asked suspiciously.

"Let me get my custom-stocked blister kit. In the meantime, sit on the car and take your shoe and sock off."

When I got back, she was sitting straight up on the trunk of the Falcon, her bare foot propped over the edge. She had a blister the size of a quarter on the back of her heel and another the size of a nickel under her big toe. They'd already burst.

I started cutting moleskin and foam rubber. "The idea," I said, "is to cut a hole in this stuff the size of your blister. First the moleskin goes on, double layer, and then the foam. I fit the holes over the blister, and then tape the pads on. That way, the blister doesn't rub against your shoe, it just touches air."

"I'm letting you do this," she said, "because I trust your instincts."

I let that go by. I certainly didn't trust my own all that much, but I felt electric currents when she said it.

"Watch out for him," Bill yelled from across camp. "He's a quack. He damn near disabled me."

She twitched when I doused the blisters with alcohol. I let her foot dry. Then I sprayed the blisters with Bactine, put on the pads, and taped her up.

She didn't limp that day, and at lunch, I sat by her and watched her sketch what was around us: a stream in a small river canyon, the rock face on the other side, the way the rocks split the running water.

"I don't know how you do that," I said. "You make rock look alive."

"I'm an expert on the inner life of rocks."

"Why didn't you study art?" I asked her, as she worked on shading with the flat of a thick Faber pencil.

"I may," she said. "I don't know if I want to stick with geology. Don't you think rocks get boring after a while?"

"It's not rocks that thrill me, but time. Rocks are just a way in."

She kissed me then, fast on the cheek, and when I looked at her, she looked straight back. "Thank you," she said.

It turned hot. One afternoon we came on an abandoned mine cut, probably close to fifty years old, given the way trees had grown in and around the tailings. I scrambled down the slope the miners had cut while following the ore, and at the bottom, where the shade was permanent, I discovered snow. It was dirty snow, composed as much of pine needles and dust as ice. Bill and Julie were right behind me.

"The start of the next period of glaciation," Bill said, just before I hit him square in the chest with a muddy ice ball. We pelted each other, and then we pelted Julie. I jumped on Bill and tried, unsuccessfully, to stuff some ice down his shirt, and Julie hopped on us both and got a handful down my back. We used up most of Michigan's next glacier.

I think we all fell in love with her, even Bill, who had nearly forgiven me for asking her to join us without consulting him. She talked with us, joked around, and even got us off the bean marathon and into a more varied diet of Rice-A-Roni, spaghetti, and Hamburger Helper. She had added her Dutch oven and saucepan to our skillet and had us doing Pillsbury rollarounds: cookie dough rolled around a stick and baked over a campfire.

And our male style was cramped somewhat. No more uninhibited farts. We deleted the word *fuck* from our working vocabularies. And what was more difficult, we barely talked about her among ourselves, not even after we'd rolled out our sleeping bags in the big tent. No one posed the question of where she fit on a scale from one to ten. She was too close, in a lot of ways.

The evening before the last day, we camped again near Marquette. I made spaghetti. We even had a salad with it and some cheap red wine.

Bill had parked the Falcon so the back end was propped on a mound of sandstone, and he was underneath it, resecuring the gas tank with a couple of clothes hangers. Carl and Evan were drinking beer. Julie was sketching while she still had light. She drew trees and rocks, but no people. Now she let everyone look through the sketch book. She'd relaxed into the role of sister or first cousin; the sadness at the base of her seemed to have eroded. I felt happy for her—and gloomy that summer was ending.

It was my turn to do the dishes, which meant washing out the cast-iron skillet and the Dutch oven. I walked down to the lake, where there was a little sandstone ledge in the water. I took off my shoes and socks, rolled up my pants, and waded in. The icy water bit at my legs with needle-sharp teeth. I grabbed a handful of sand and scrubbed away, trying to finish before my toes went numb.

"Are you freezing?" I heard behind me.

"Hi, Julie," I said. "Have you ever gone swimming in Lake Superior?"

"Never. I thought it was impossible." The evening wind plucked at the short tufts of her hair as if they were feathers.

"I think it's impossible to stand in two feet of it." I got out. The veins in my legs stood out in bold, blue relief.

"That really works, doesn't it?"

"The sand? Sure. Best way to clean anything—even yourself."

We sat down on the bank and looked out at the lake. It was almost dark.

"Do you like it out here? You seem to."

"It's been nice. I'm glad you guys invited me. You're gentlemen, all of you." She looked down at the sand.

I said, "You know, this year in classes, sometimes, I watched you out of the corner of my eye."

"I thought you did. Once in a while."

"You seemed sad."

"Really?"

"Sometimes you'd smile at people, and then, right after, you'd seem sadder than ever. You worried me."

"Really? Why?"

"I don't know," I said. "I just felt that way."

"You probably don't remember," she said. "One day I saw you in the laundry room? At Douglas Houghton Hall?"

"With Rasmussen."

"God. You do remember."

"I thought he was going to hit you."

"I was breaking up with him. Well, it was more complicated than that. We went together for a while when I was a freshman, and broke up, and then he wanted to get back together when I came back, and . . . God, what a mess. You guys have all been so nice."

"Why did you take that year off? I'm glad you did. Otherwise I wouldn't have had the chance to get to know you."

"I didn't exactly take it off." She looked down, scooped up some sand, and let it slide through her fingers. "I may transfer. Art. Maybe I'd be a good medical illustrator. I like precision."

"You draw beautiful coelenterates," I said. "I hope you don't transfer."

She smiled weakly. "You thought I looked sad, huh?"

"Yeah."

"The last two years have been hard for me. I guess it comes out when I'm not watching."

We were silent for a long time.

"I had cancer last year," she whispered. "That's why I was gone. I was scared I was going to die. I had radiation. I lost my hair. It was really long, and it grew back like this. When I came back to school, I kept it short, like it had been my decision."

She struggled to say something, but couldn't. An awful, hollow sound came out of her, and she began to sob. I put my arms around her. She sobbed until her whole body shook. I held her and ran my hand over her hair. Finally, she cried herself into silence.

We listened to the lake slapping against the sandstone and to the wind swooshing through the pine boughs. The northern sky had gone to midnight blue.

"That's not all," she said finally. "I didn't just lose my hair for a while. I lost a breast. Do you know how rare that is in a woman my age? It's practically unheard of. Like God came down and touched me. Sometimes I thought about killing myself."

"Julie."

She took my hand and put it on her left breast. "Push."

I did, a little.

"Harder." She put her hands over mine to help.

Her bra collapsed under my hand. It was stiff, but hollow, and she held my hand there for a while. Then she guided my hand to her right breast and pushed it against herself. "There," she said. "Go ahead."

I felt the contour, the soft weight that I should have felt on the other side.

"That's what I lost," she said. "But as bad as that was, now I think more about the cancer coming back and killing me piece by piece. Do you believe in God?"

"No."

"I don't, either. I did, but it made everything worse."

"Julie, maybe this is a stupid thing to say, but you're alive. You're healthy. . . ."

"I don't know. Maybe we are just exactly our bodies, from our toes to our brains. And I've lost part of myself."

She touched my knee, got up, and walked back to camp. Instead of staying up with us that night, as she usually did, talking by the fire, she went to bed.

The next morning, mapping, we sweated down to our belts. We didn't have enough to drink to stay hydrated, and that put us on edge. Besides, Bill, Carl, and Evan had heard her cry. They'd seen the way she'd gone to bed, and I hadn't told them anything. I kept wanting to talk to Julie, to say something that would help, but I had no opportunity to be alone with her. What could I say that wouldn't sound superficial? Anyway, maybe attention was not what she wanted now.

At midafternoon, we drove through L'Anse; the electric sign at Michigan National Bank read ninety-eight degrees. Nordeng drove the lead car, taking us out to the tip of the Huron Peninsula, Point Abbaye. We traveled on logging roads with big ruts. Carl drove. I bounced around in the backseat with Bill and Julie. I wondered when some rock in the middle of the road would gut Bill's Falcon. Bill didn't seem to care.

"God, would I like a shower," Julie said. "I must smell like a goat."

She was still wearing a flannel shirt, but for the first time she'd loosened the top two buttons. Rivulets of sweat coursed down the hollow of her throat. Bill and I sat in our soaked white T-shirts. Carl's hair stood out, plastered at odd angles. Even the breeze through the windows couldn't dry us or strip away the layers of pine smoke, sweat, and caked-on grime we wore.

"Deodorant is unnecessary," Bill said. "You just get used to human odors."

"The olfactory nerves go numb," I said.

"Not mine," Julie replied.

As we traveled northeast, along the skeletal finger of land, we could see water, first on one side, then the other, through odd breaks in the trees. When we got to the point, the sky was lowering, threatening rain but not following through. We piled stiffly out of the car. To the west was Keewenaw Bay and way across, the Keewenaw Peninsula, part of a huge geosyncline that surfaced again at Isle Royale, on the other side of Lake Superior. To the east was Huron Bay and close and huge, as if magnified by the thickening air, the black Huron Mountains.

Nordeng gathered us in a circle. "I want you to just walk around," he said. "Take a good look at this place. You don't have to map it. You don't have to draw it, unless you want to." He looked at Julie; he was in love with her drawings. "Take a half hour. Then tell me what happened here and when it happened."

We were on a dark slab of shale. It was brushy, and sand filled some of the low spots. I walked to the edge of the water and looked down. I could see clear to the flat, yellow rock that made up the bottom.

The depth looked to be about four feet, though it was hard to tell. I put my hand in, expecting that bone-numbing Lake Superior chill, and found the water pleasantly cool. I wondered how far out the rock bottom extended.

Bill crouched beside me, put his hand in, and splashed his face. He looked at me in disbelief. "We could go swimming in this!"

"The water's just shallow enough to get warm here," I said. "That rock must go out for a long way. Maybe miles."

I scouted on my own through the bushes, roaming around, looking for anything out of the ordinary. I found the charcoal remains of a campfire, rusted Schlitz and Old Milwaukee cans on a pile of burned wood. A few minutes later, I found Julie with several other students, sitting next to a large hunk of petrified snot. It was globular, yellowish green, about the size of a softball, with a tendril of smaller snot bubbles attached to it.

I sat beside her. "What the hell is that?" I said.

"I don't know. But I think it's what Dr. Nordeng wants us to puzzle over."

"We're going swimming once this is all done. The water out here is beautiful. You want to come?"

She looked at me with disbelief and whispered: "I didn't bring a bathing suit. I haven't even got a bathing suit. And . . . you know."

"I'm going in clothes and all. I just want to cool off. And it'll feel good," I whispered back, grinning.

She was sketching whatever it was, contrasting it with the dark rock in which it was embedded. There was another one a few feet away. It entered at the edge of her drawing. "I ought to know

what this is," she said. "I'm sure I've seen something like it before."

I tried to scratch it with my jackknife, but I just left part of the
knife on the rock. "It's like quartz. Chert. That's why it's still here.
It's the toughest thing around. Probably the rest of this shale just
wore away around it. What would cause a quartz bubble?"

"Maybe it's a fossil."

"Made out of silica?"

"Like petrified wood."

I just stared at it. "I don't remember it from paleo."

Eventually, Carl, Evan, and Bill walked up. They had no idea,
either. We all walked around Point Abbaye like a flock of pigeons,
stupidly bobbing our heads up and down, staring at globes and
strings of petrified gunk.

Finally, Nordeng pulled us together. He was dressed all in
green, workshirt and pants, and he had big Wolverine boots on,
the kind I wore to go deer hunting. His magnifying glass hung
from a rawhide bootlace, and his white-blond crew cut glowed,
as did the perspiration on his jowls. "Any ideas what these knobs
are?"

No one said a word, but Nordeng was in no hurry. He let us
stew.

After several minutes he said, "Stromatolites. Layered masses
of bacteria and sediment. You're looking at one of the earliest
forms of life. So what must this place have been like?"

"A shallow sea," Julie said. "Cambrian? Early Cambrian?"

"Precambrian. The old bones of the planet. And what are these
globs made of?"

"Silica. Like quartz," one of the other students offered.

"How did that happen?" Nordeng looked at me.

"I suppose the stromatolites were buried, maybe in some kind
of mudflow—this shale here. And in that mudflow, there was a
silicate solution that replaced the bacteria?"

"I want you all to keep thinking about it. Write an explanation;
you can put it in my box on Monday. Anybody here ever read
Thomas Browne?"

Nobody raised a hand.

"You should read him someday. Textbooks and the sports page aren't everything. He wrote a book called *Religio Medici*. He said we're all just 'a small parenthesis in eternity.' From beginning to end, maybe life itself is just a footnote in time. What's three and a half billion years in this universe?" He looked down at the stromatolites. "Respect these things. You're related."

We stood silent, looking down at the blobs as if we were at a prayer meeting. Eventually people started walking back to their cars. A few students talked to Nordeng. The sun was breaking through in the west, lighting up the enormous dark clouds and mountains in the east, polarizing the world in shadow and gold; pine boughs became iridescent, and the water flattened to dead calm.

"Julie?" I said. "Do you want to swim?"

"I don't think so," she said. "I'll catch a ride back with Dr. Nordeng. Could you hang onto my tent and backpack?"

"Sure," I said. Then I smiled at her. "I'll see you Monday? Let me know when you want the camping stuff."

"This is the strangest place I've ever seen," she said.

When we heard the cars leaving, we peeled off our clothes: four animals, red-faced, white-bellied, and sticky. Light sheared across the surface of the lake. I dove, and as I skimmed over the bottom, the oppression of heat, the need to think and theorize, measure and worry, all washed away. The water was cool, practically effervescent, and the rock bottom was made of coarse sandstone, rilled and petrified into little dunes. I stood up, and the water came to the middle of my chest. Looking down, I could see each wrinkle in my toes. I ran the soles of my feet over the sandstone, savoring the touch. We walked out a long way, toward the Keewenaw Peninsula, and the depth never varied. We surfaced and dove, sinuous and slick as dolphins. The sea of the stromatolites must have been something like this, I thought, but murkier, tidal, and salty. I was in the crystal element, the north, and I dove again and again, eyes wide to each shift of light. All my sins had been forgiven in advance; my impediments and infirmities, weaknesses and limitations, were all absolved, not by God, but by time. We must have been sixty or seventy yards offshore, with no change in depth, when I decided to break off on my own. I slowly backstroked toward the shore, and when I got tired, stood up and turned.

She stood on the rock where we'd left our clothes. She was naked, and I almost turned away to let her have that brief second of privacy before she dove in and wrapped the water around her. But I couldn't. She was perfect: her knees bent, thighs tensed to make the dive, the line of her back and hips, one curve. She barely disturbed the water when she dove, and she came up laughing, her black hair plastered against her head like a seal's.

I walked toward her, scuffing my toes against the sandstone ridges. She came toward me, shining and smooth, and the scar where her breast had been trembled in the water like a thin flame.

A Knight Pursued

Mark Altschuler awoke, priapic with yearning for his wife, or perhaps, he had to admit, for women in general: after all, what did hormone fluctuations know about loyalty? The room was lit only by a digital clock, whose big numbers splashed crimson on the walls: 3:10. He stared at the ceiling, lying at attention, arms at his sides, not wanting to bump Mary. She breathed softly, asleep, balanced as precariously on her side of the small Murphy bed as he on his.

She'd been reading the diaries of William Byrd and had picked up the plantation owner's eighteenth-century lingo: a few nights before she'd pulled Mark into bed and said, "Roger me, darling. Give the old wife a flourish." Then she'd overlaid Byrd with an imitation of Hemingway's Bret Ashley: "I say, give a chap a roger. Can't a chap get rogered around here?" Mary had a way of turning most things into a joke, but the night before, switching to biblical mode, she had said with complete seriousness, "I want to be gotten with child." She thought they should get started on it as soon as possible. This both scared the bejesus out of Mark and awakened his desire.

He hadn't slept more than four or five hours a night in weeks, and preoccupation with his internship had given him an indifference to lovemaking that, a couple months before, he would have thought impossible. Mary's yearning to start a family before either of them had decent jobs made his insomnia marginally worse by stirring him up and giving him another issue to think about. But mainly, as he lay in bed, he thought about everything he should have done differently in court the day before and everything that might go wrong the coming day.

At 5:00 he gave up. The weather had been usually warm for Seattle, and he felt sticky. Barely enough gray light seeped into the apartment to outline the jumbled furniture. The bed, small as it was, took up most of the room. Two stuffed chairs, a sofa, an end table, a standing lamp—all of which had come with the apartment—were wedged between the bed and the wall, as if pushed there by a glacier. Mark eased himself out of bed and teetered across the moraine. On the other side he congratulated himself on not upsetting a lamp or breaking his neck, closed the bathroom door, and turned on the light. There was no shower, just a big claw-foot bathtub. He used a washcloth, running water in the sink at a trickle to keep the noise down. He put on his suit in the walk-in closet across from the bathroom and stepped back into the hall, cracking the closet door so he had a little light. Mary was still asleep, but his files were across the room, stacked on the dinette. He cursed himself for not bringing them on the first trip.

As he swung a leg over the sofa, balancing on a shelf of books, Mary rolled onto her back. He made it to the files, which stood six inches deep on the table. He'd have to make it over the furniture once more, this time one-handed. Going back, he nearly dropped the files, all forty-one of them, which, though pressed tightly to his side, were fanning out. He fell back against the cinder block-and-plank bookshelves and felt them lean with him to the right. Planks slid, cinder blocks thudded, and books slapped around his feet. He extricated a foot and put it down. Bindings crunched as he skidded on the down slope of paperback covers. A Dürer print, "A Knight Pursued by Death and the Devil," hit the floor, and glass broke.

Mary moaned a little and sat up, eyelids fluttering. Her hair fell in dark shadows around her face and over her nightgown. She arched her back, trying to come awake, and Mark, who loved to watch her move, thought that, even half-conscious, she was splendid.

Mary usually slept soundly and deeply, yet, some small part of her always took note of Mark's nocturnal thrashings, and she vaguely registered him, somewhere at the foot of the bed, groping around like a bear in a garbage dump. "What time is it?" she asked.

"A little past 5:00."

"Uhh . . . And I thought I was going to escape the farm."

The mattress sagged when he sat beside her.

"I knocked over the books," he said.

"We've got too many. They're getting in the way of life. You'll break your neck, and then you'll never get me pregnant." She rubbed her eyes.

"I was hoping that after a good night's sleep you'd come to your senses."

"I didn't get a good night's sleep. When did you wake up?"

"3:00."

"Did you get back to sleep?"

"No."

"What is it Mark?"

"I wake up thinking of cross-examinations. It'll go away, eventually. Habit's a great deadener."

She crooked her arms around his neck and, squeezing, pulled him down until they were nose to nose.

"This is fate. We're both awake. It's almost dawn. Let's make a baby. . . ."

Mark shook his head as much as he could in the vise grips.

"Where were you going?" she asked.

"Denny's. I didn't want to wake you up, and I was tired of lying there, staring at the ceiling. Then I'm giving Paula Pierson a ride in. Her car's in the shop. We've got the morning calendar in Everett District Court."

"Come back to bed."

"Mary. . . ."

"OK. No more. I'll make coffee." She rolled out of bed and flicked on the overhead light, which staggered them both. While she put the Murphy bed up and made coffee and toast, Mark put the furniture in order and fumbled with books.

"I think we should sell some books," she said. "We filled half the U-Haul with them when we left Michigan, and how many will we ever read again? Do you mind if I do some culling?"

"No."

"Just leave them on the floor. I never used to think that a person could read too much. Now I'm beginning to change my mind."

"Wrong attitude," Mark pronounced, sitting down at the dinette, his files next to him on the floor. "Wrong attitude for a graduate student."

"But it's true. Books are supposed to enhance life. Not replace it."

"You shouldn't have gone to summer school," he said. "You needed a break."

"I need to connect with what my professors laughingly refer to as 'the real world.' They always say it with quotation marks, as if there weren't one. I, however, hold out for the real world—I believe in it."

"I'm up to my ears in it. I hold for escapism."

The coffee stopped dripping, and she poured them some. "What's your morning calendar like?"

"Light." He reached into his files and passed her a smeary photocopy. At the top it said "Everett District Court, August 7, 1977." Underneath, thirteen cases were listed with charges: DWI, physical control, negligent driving, speeding.

"For an intern, they sure give you a lot of work."

They finished breakfast, and Mary kissed her husband goodbye. She liked the farm better, where work and home occupied the same place.

When she turned to the pile of books, she noticed Mark's print had hit the floor. The glass was cracked. She leaned the frame gently against the wall and started sorting the books into two piles.

Mary had spent the previous day reading *As You Like It* for her Shakespeare course. She read it slowly, a mug of coffee within easy reach, pausing over lines, speaking some of them aloud, giving herself over to the sensual music of Shakespeare's green world. As Rosalind moved toward marriage and all it implied, Mary felt the jumble inside herself rearrange and come together, like a Rubik's Cube that had solved itself.

Mark returned from Everett just after she finished the play. She twined her arms around his neck, stood on tiptoe, and kissed him for a long time. Then, without a word, she went into the kitchen and started breaking eggs into the frying pan.

"Did you know," she called, "that Shakespeare's mother was named Mary Arden? And that she lived near the forest of Arden? That she came from a strong Catholic family and that Arden forest is where *As You Like It* takes place, mainly?"

"No."

"And that Arden can also be taken as the forest of Ardennes, in France? I read the play again for Shakespeare tonight. I was going to read it fast so I could get to the stuff for theory, but I wanted to read slowly for a change. So I took all day. I realized that reading had become a desperate act for me."

"Welcome to grad school."

"I don't even know why I read the plays for that class. We never talk about them—we just sit around the table and use Shakespeare as a political launchpad."

Mary went to the seminar at 7:00, and it was as bad as she had thought it would be, all politics, patriarchy, and linguistic absurdities, but not a word about the beauty of the play or any light that it had to shed on love or the human condition. Nothing that had excited her about literature was alive in any of her classes.

At 10:00, Mark was waiting for her outside Padelford Hall to walk her home. He was there every night she went to class and every evening she finished her receptionist job at the hotel. Buildings and old-fashioned streetlights lit the campus and sent shadows in every direction. She inserted her fingers through Mark's and kissed him.

"Are you here because you love me, or are you here to protect your patriarchal goodies?" she said.

"Huh?"

"Are men in general terrified of female sexual power?"

"Well, I always have been."

"Let's devise sports. What think you of falling in love?"

"I thought we were in love. At least you led me to believe so."

"I loved you not," she said.

"I was the more deceived."

"We are arrant knaves, all; believe none of us."

"There's no following you in this fierce vein—and that's the truth. I don't even know why you bother to read Shakespeare anymore. You've got him memorized."

"I can't help it. The lines just stick. Where were we?"

"'I thought we were in love.'"

"Yes. That thou didst know how many fathoms deep I am in love. What thinkest thou of having babies?"

"I think'st it's a good idea, say, five or six years from now."

"I'll be thirty if we wait six years. Do you know that we are living for the first time in history that marriage no longer entails childbearing? When people took wedding vows in the past, childbed was just around the corner. Making a baby was the way people ratified their wedding vows. In a way, we're not even married. Mark, I want to be married."

"We are."

"We haven't done the most intimate thing yet."

"And that would be?"

"Fucking for real."

"What exactly have we been doing?"

"I mean no pills and no rubbers." She bowed her head, gazed up at him, and smiled softly.

"God, don't *do* that." He looked away. "I've got another year of law school. I don't know whether I'll get a job. You've got at least four more to get a doctorate. We need to get our feet on the ground before we have kids."

"Maybe it's stupid to try to control life that much. We've always had it so planned. I want to be gotten with child. By you."

"What about your M.A.?"

"I don't think I can take it anymore. I can't use 'foreground' as a verb without flinching."

Paula Pierson was a public defender, and nominally Mark's adversary, but PDs and prosecutors usually worked together to achieve reasonable results, and Mark had come to see her as a colleague and friend. He pulled into her driveway at 7:15. The house was a bungalow with a little front yard of scorched grass and three or four struggling dandelions. The *Seattle Post-Intelligencer* was sitting on the porch, and he picked it up. "Carter OKs Neutron Bomb," the headline read. Progress was being made every day. Mark tentatively rang the doorbell. It was the buzzer type, and it let go like a fire alarm.

There was some thumping, and Paula opened the door, dressed in her usual tailored outfit, mug of coffee in hand. "Hi. Do you want a cup of coffee?"

She shoved the mug at him.

"Frank's downstairs. I'm going to tell him we're off. Come on, I'll introduce you."

Paula clattered downstairs, doing a great balancing act on her heels. She stood in the basement, in front of a closed door. "I'm going. Be back about 6:00. What about you?"

"7:00 or 8:00," came the voice from the other side.

"Frank, I want you to meet Mark."

"Hi Mark," Frank said.

"Hi."

"Frank hasn't got any clothes on," Paula said. "He's trying to get the pilot light on the water heater fixed."

"Oh," Mark said.

"So I guess your introduction will have to be verbal."

"Nice to meet you Frank," Mark said to the door.

"Same here," Frank said.

"I took a cold shower this morning. It was murder. Frank is dedicated to hot water. See you later," she called.

"Later," Frank said.

Mark felt a little embarrassed driving with Paula into Everett. Despite her suit, which was creased and flat in all the right places, some of her husband's nakedness still clung to her, and therefore, suggested some of her own.

Mary put her hair in a fast ponytail, pulled on running shorts, a jog bra, and a T-shirt, and hauled the cinder blocks and planks down to the alley by the Cafe Espresso. She set the planks on the blocks, as they had been in the apartment, went into the cafe, and told the cashier, "There's free bookshelves out there for anyone who wants them." Outside, she planted one foot, at waist level, against the red brick wall. She put her head to her knee without too much strain. She did the same with the other leg, getting a good stretch in her groin and hamstrings. Then she started to jog, down the Ave, to the Burke Gilman Trail.

She tried to get in three or four runs a week. She hated the first few minutes, when she felt dizzy and stiff. But as she got into her stride, ligament, tendon, and muscle loosened and glided past one another with well-lubricated efficiency. She had long, strong legs and sound knees. When she ran, she took long strides, and the muscles on the outsides of her thighs flowed under her skin; she could feel her ponytail bounce and fly off the back of her neck. By the time she broke sweat on the first quarter mile of the trail, she would be gliding.

The week had been unusually hot, but the morning air was cool, and she ran down the Ave, across the Campus Parkway, and turned west, heading toward the marinas and Gasworks Park. Soon the trail gave way to normal sidewalk. The streets were filling. The traffic on Pacific headed east in the direction of the University Hospital and the Montlake Bridge. She saw the stream of cars on the University and I-5 bridges. Pedestrians crossed her path and got out of the way as she entered a shady stretch. She began to feel loose and warm. Maybe she'd go all the way to Gasworks. She passed the Northlake Tavern at a dead run, stretching, striding out, airborne, and then she saw the dog.

It was longhaired, black and brown, maybe part Australian shepherd, part shelty, a good farm dog, the kind that liked to go for strangers' ankles. But it acted cosmopolitan and harmless enough, sidling across the intersection with a rakish bent to its ears, tail high, tongue lolling out of a big, sloppy grin.

The car that hit the dog was a blue rust bucket of an Oldsmobile, moving fast off Sixth onto Northlake. As it turned, the corner of the right bumper caught the dog smartly on the shoulder. The dog gave a fraction of a yelp; Mary gasped, thinking it would go under the wheel, but the car, which neither swerved nor slowed, had hit the dog hard enough to knock it clear. She stopped, trying to get air after her sprint, and watched the car speed away. The dog lay near the side of the street like a bunched-up towel.

Mary checked for cars and ran to the dog. It had a red gash on its shoulder where the hair was matted and sticky with blood. She caressed it behind one ear. It rolled its eyes toward her and whined. She looked down the street toward Gasworks and then back toward the hospital, as if merely looking could conjure up two white-suited men with a stretcher. The dog turned its head a little and licked her hand. A car went past close enough to make Mary's hair blow, and she jerked away.

The dog was medium-sized, male, maybe thirty or forty pounds. It had no collar. Mary was afraid to pick it up: what if its back were injured or it had a cracked rib? But leaving it in the street would be worse. The Offshore Grill didn't look open. Nothing would be open down by the lake except maybe the marinas farther back on Pacific. She thought she could carry it that far. She saw a car coming, looked up, and waved her arm. The car went by, going into the other lane to get around. She knelt down in back of the dog and slid her right arm underneath its forequarters. The pavement ground into her knees. She got her left arm underneath the hindquarters.

She used her arms like a forklift, and once she had the dog as high as her chest, stood up. It was an awkward move, unbalanced, and she felt the stretch in her back muscles and pressure in her knees as she wobbled to her feet.

The dog whined a little more but took it calmly enough. Another car came down Northlake, and Mary half-said, half-mouthed, "Help!" The car went by. Who wanted to pick up a bloody dog and a sweaty jogger when they were already running late?

She tried the Offshore Grill, but it was closed. A sign in the window said, "Staff on vacation this week." She made for the marinas at a steady pace, trying not to jar the dog, which made no move but to lick at her once in a while. Blood had smeared her T-shirt.

Mary crossed to the south side of the road and started walking east. Cars went over her head on I-5. Gravel crunched under her feet where the sidewalk disappeared. An overgrown thicket of blackberry bushes on her right clawed at her like a nest of fishhooks. She just bulled ahead. The thorns dug into her T-shirt and her flesh, pulled, and finally let go with a snap. The sidewalk reappeared. Cars blew by.

She made it to the marinas, down a long driveway and into the parking lot; her arms and neck ached. The marinas seemed deserted. She walked out onto the pier and noticed a gas pump. "Hello?" she called. "Is anybody out there?" No one answered.

She went to a store with life preservers and rain slickers in the window. The door was locked, but a light was on in the back. She had no free hand, so she kicked at the door. Way in the back, a man stuck his head into the light. She kicked the door again, harder. The man disappeared. The sign on the door said, "Open 10:00–7:00."

"Damn it," she muttered to herself and then shrieked, "BASTARD!"

The dog looked up at her in alarm.

"I'll take care of this myself," she muttered. She'd seen a sign for a pet clinic at a shopping center called University Village. She guessed it was about two, three miles away.

It took her twenty minutes of fast, grim walking to get as far as the University Hospital. Her arms quivered. She didn't look left or right, didn't make eye contact with pedestrian or driver, and did not stop at corners. At Fifteenth and Pacific, she could tell that a big white van was going for a quick right-hand turn, despite the fact that she had a "Walk" light. She just went into the street and forced it to a rubber-sizzling halt. The bumper stopped inches from her hip. The driver gaped, slack-jawed, at the girl with the hard legs, bloody T-shirt and comatose dog. She scattered a group of medical students coming over from the campus to the hospital. By the time she got to the pet clinic, the muscles in her upper body had turned to molten iron.

"Oh, the poor thing," the lady behind the desk said. "What's its name?"

"I don't know. He hasn't got a collar."

"Isn't he your dog?"

"No."

"Here," she said, opening a door, "bring him back in here and we'll get him on a table and have Dr. Adair look at him."

Mary put the dog on a table, and straightened her frozen arms. Sweet pain coursed from her back and neck to her fingertips.

"I'm Susan Adair," Mary heard from behind. She turned and there, apparently, was the vet. She stood two heads shorter than Mary, and her fine blonde hair brushed her ears and neck. She smiled cheerfully and stroked the dog's head. "Got hit by a car?" she said to the dog, who licked her hand: "You're a sweet-tempered guy, aren't you?"

Mary felt better just being close to this woman. She was calm, but alert as a sandpiper.

"I just saw him get hit. I was jogging down by the I-5 bridge."

"The I-5 bridge? You carried him from there to here?"

"Cars just kept going by."

Adair probed the dog's leg lightly with her fingers.

"Broken leg, I think." Adair left the room and returned with a syringe and a bottle.

"We'll give him some potassium chloride for shock, and then we'll give him an X ray. You carried that dog a long way."

"Comes from years of baling hay."

"You baled hay?"

"My dad's got a dairy farm in Michigan."

"No kidding? I grew up on a dairy farm near Puyallup. Wasn't much at baling hay, though. Too short and skinny."

Adair left with the dog to take X rays. Its front right leg was broken near the shoulder.

"Do you think he'll be all right?" Mary asked.

"Sure. I can put a cast on him. The leg will mend. Do you want to take him home with you?"

"I can't. I live in an apartment. No pets allowed. I smuggled in a rat, but a dog. . . ."

"I can't keep him. I'd be up to my ears in stray dogs. I probably shouldn't even be treating him. I don't own this place—just work here."

"I'll pay."

"But then what? What will you do with him?"

"What do you think I should I do?"

"The first thing is to look for the owner. Put signs up in the area where you saw him get hit, maybe around the U-District. The pound won't take an animal injured this badly. They can't care for it. They haven't got all that much money or room, and nobody wants to adopt a dog with a broken leg. Same with the SPCA. It isn't that they wouldn't like to help, but they're overwhelmed with healthy animals. Do you know anyone who'd want a dog?"

"What happens to those dogs? The injured ones?"

"Stray dogs with an injury like this, they usually just put them to sleep."

Mary thought of Mark and their ever-depleted checking account. "How much will all this cost?"

"If you decide you want to put him to sleep, I'll call the SPCA and they'll do it for nothing. I won't even charge you for the X rays, given the effort you put into getting him here."

"Thanks."

"Do you want to do that? Or are there other options?"

"God." Mary wracked her brains. Let the dog get better? Put it in a crate and send it back home? Her dad could pick him up at Tri-City airport.

Mary just said, "I'll make sure you get paid. For the X rays too."

"What are you thinking of doing?"

"If I can't find who he belongs to? Sending him home. Home to Michigan. God. I wonder how much an airline would charge."

Between the two of them, Mark and Paula had cleared the morning calendar by 11:00, plea bargain after plea bargain. "You want to get a cup of coffee?" Paula asked.

"You bet," he said.

They walked out of the building, strolled a few blocks to Karl's Bakery, and found a table. Paula was built on a more delicate scale than Mary. She had slim legs, encased in dark nylon. She was in the habit of crossing and uncrossing them, and as she did so, nylon rubbed on nylon and played an anthem that made Mark feel uncomfortable with his thoughts. He found himself wanting to run his fingers from her knees to her ankles, just to hear the zip.

"How are you doing?" she asked. "You seem a bit fagged out."

"Oh. Just a little trouble sleeping."

"The legal intern jitters?"

"That's it," he laughed. "If it's so obvious, I guess I'm in trouble."

"No, you're doing great."

Mark thought a moment. He preferred to keep his life with Mary to himself, but this morning he felt compelled to seek a second opinion.

"Mary and I have been thinking about having kids."

"You're kidding."

"What makes you think so?"

"You're so young. I mean, not *that* young. But Mark, you haven't even got a real job yet. You're a Rule 9 intern. You have to think about getting your career settled first."

"I guess so."

"And Mary's getting a Ph.D., right?"

"Maybe."

"Maybe?"

"I just don't see her making it."

"Why not?"

"She can't help finding her professors ridiculous."

"What would she do?"

"I don't know. Be a mother, I guess."

Paula shook her head, as if she were trying to clear it. "Well, I've thought about kids. I can still have them. I mean it's getting a little late, but lots of women are waiting longer. . . . I just made other choices, none of which I regret. . . . I mean you *can* have kids early, but nobody I know. . . ."

"It's a different choice for everybody," Mark offered.

"Actually, Mark, I'm getting divorced. I'm glad kids aren't involved."

"Wow," he said softly. Up flashed the image of a squatting, naked, generic male trying to fix the pilot light on a water heater.

"Yes, wow. I'm a little miserable. I keep shuffling it around. It just didn't work out. His whole life revolved around making partner, and now, he's not going to make it. You'd think someone shot him in the knees, the way he carries on. It's not like he doesn't have other options, other firms that would be glad to have him."

"That's too bad."

"He's a good lawyer. He'll make a good move. It's not the end of the world for him."

"I mean about your marriage."

"Oh," she laughed. "No, I'm relieved, really. We're going in different directions. Somebody finally made a decision—me. We're still friends. Frank will move out in a month or so. He'll get on with his life, and I'll get on with mine."

"But you feel a little miserable."

"Yes," she said. "I sure do." She reached across the table and squeezed his hand.

Mary walked from the pet clinic to the administration building. She was a mess of sweat and blood, but the ad building was on the way home, and she decided she did not have time to walk to the apartment, clean up, and come back. She asked the woman behind the window for forms to withdraw from summer quarter.

"I'm sorry," she said, "but it's too late to withdraw. The deadline was last week."

"You mean I'm stuck? I can't get out even if I want to?"

"You just need to get special permission."

"Let me get this straight. I'm twenty-four. I voted in the last election. I earn money working fifteen hours a week as a hotel receptionist, and I pay for my tuition with it. I understand the money's gone, but you're telling me I need special permission just to leave this place? Whose permission do I need?"

"Your instructors' and your dean's."

"What if I just leave? Drop out?"

"Well, you'll fail your classes for the quarter. Why don't you just take these cards and get the signatures? They always give permission."

"I don't think I should have to get anyone's permission. I think it's up to me. Period."

"Look," the woman said tiredly, "I just work here."

"I'm sorry."

The woman waved it off. Mary decided that if the university thought she needed its permission, that was the university's problem. She was tired and her arms and back ached. Tomorrow she'd put up signs about the dog. Now she hoped she could make enough money from the books to pay for his X rays.

Mary went back up to the apartment and ran the hottest water she could stand into the bathtub. She slid in until her head went under, and stayed there as long as she could. The blackberry scratches stung, especially on her right shoulder, which had been thoroughly slashed. Her arm muscles felt like they contained ground glass. She came up, blowing the air out of her lungs slowly and deliberately. Then she closed her eyes and sank under again. After her bath, she went to the used book store, got some boxes, and spent an hour sorting books and carting them up and down the stairs. The old woman behind the cash register reluctantly paid her $73.50 for the lot.

⊷ ⩵◈⩵ ⊶

Mark was struggling against afternoon drowsiness when Phil Gifford came into the library. Gifford was tall and curly-haired, and he wore horn-rimmed glasses. He had a wide smile, and Mark wondered what he found so amusing.

"Whatcha up to?" Gifford asked.

"Not much."

"Want to see an autopsy?"

"Sure." An autopsy?

"Leave your jacket here. It's hot."

Mark had only seen two dead people in his whole life, both in nicely beflowered funeral parlors.

They passed the county law library and stopped at the elevators. Gifford tapped his toe while they waited. "It's in the basement," he offered. They took the elevator down one floor and got out into a small brightly lit area of high-gloss white walls and linoleum. The fluorescent light bounced around the corridor, and an aura formed around Gifford's white shirt and teeth.

Mark followed him down the short hall to a glass door. Gifford unlocked it, and they stepped out into a dimly lit underground garage. Three white vans were parked off to the left, and the place smelled of gasoline and tires. Gifford went to the right, across a small loading bay, toward a white door. "That's the cutting room," Gifford said. He opened the door, and Mark followed him in.

Mark heard the fan and felt as much as smelled the oily stench emanating from inside. Two men were in the room. One was conducting the autopsy. He had a shiny, nearly bald head, dewed with sweat and fringed with curling white hair. He wore dark pants, a white shirt, and a big plastic lab apron that tied at the back of his neck and at his waist. A uniformed county cop, short and chubby, stood next to the medical examiner. The cop wore a short-sleeved shirt, and his thick forearms were covered with long carroty hair. A huge fan blew across the table where the medical examiner worked, creating a cyclone of sweet stench. It may have provided the examiner with some relief, but Mark almost gagged.

What was left of a woman was on the stainless steel table. Fluids leaked from her swollen legs. The coroner was sawing off her head.

Mark wedged himself into a corner of the cramped room, backed against some cabinets and a sink. The woman's head lolled as the saw bit in. Mark looked into the holes in her face, where her eyes had melted away. The secret to getting through this would be not thinking. Stay on the surface of it and glide. Don't get sick. Don't think. Just float.

The saw thrusts across the trachea were easy, but then the doctor hit the neck bone and had to bear down. Mark couldn't take his eyes away. Gifford must have noticed a quizzical expression on his face because he explained, "We've got no idea who she is. So we cut off the head and hands and send them to the FBI. Maybe they can give us an ID from dental records or fingerprints."

Mark muttered, "Looks like she's been dead a while."

"Probably about a week," the examiner said. "Ninety-degree weather."

"Some kids found her this morning," Gifford said. "They were riding their bikes around out on a county road and stopped to pick blackberries. They found her in the bushes. She'd been shot through the head seven times—.22 caliber bullets."

Once the head was removed, the corpse was a little easier to look at, a little less human. Still, Mark felt embarrassed for her, embarrassed to be looking at all. Aside from Mary, she was the only woman he'd ever seen naked. When he and Mary were naked together, even when they made love, there was an essential modesty between them. Mark valued that shyness. It made them careful of each other. The remains on the table had no modesty left, and having none, seemed to suck it, like a vacuum, from the men in the room.

Streaks of green and purple ran up her legs and arms and into her torso. Her breasts were burst and flat, her pubic region green, the hair falling out in clumps. She was awash in maggots, a writhing white foam that flowed onto the table and dripped onto the floor. They fed on her and on the oil that seeped from her. As the coroner and the cop shifted the body, the maggots flowed over their gloves.

The doctor sawed off the left hand and then the right. Mark thought it was worse than watching the head come off, as if there were more humanity in the hands. A maggot crawled onto the cop's finger. He flicked it toward Mark and laughed. "Nasty little things."

"Have you looked at her back?" Gifford asked.

"No," the coroner said.

"We'd better turn her over."

The coroner stared back at Gifford. It was clear he'd had enough.

"We'd feel awfully embarrassed," Gifford said, "if there was a knife wound in the back, and we missed it."

Gifford waited.

"Mark, can you give me some help? Dr. Hanson's been at this a long while—we'll give him a hand."

Gifford himself put on a pair of surgical gloves and an apron, and Mark followed suit. Mark took her by the shoulders while Gifford grabbed her hips, and they tried to turn her, but she was so slick and heavy—like squishy rubber—that they both had to exert all their strength to hang on and flip her. Mark's forearm skidded on the greasy table.

There was no knife in her back and no wound.

"OK," Gifford said. "We'll let you gentlemen finish up." He and Mark stripped off the gloves and washed their hands. Mark soaped and rinsed his forearm but wished for a Brillo pad to scrub it. "Ready?" Gifford said lightly.

Walking back up the stairs, Gifford said, "Ya done good. That was a tough one. If you stick with this job you're going to see ugly crime scenes, all kinds of god-awful stuff. Might as well find out if you can take it."

Mark nodded his head dumbly. "Do you have any ideas about who killed her?"

"So far," Gifford said, "not a clue."

Mary trudged upstairs from the bookstore and got cleaned up for work. She tossed her birth control pills in the wastebasket, went to a drugstore, bought some Trojan-Enz—at least she wouldn't be wondering what was happening to her body—and walked to the hotel. She was halfway through her shift at the Nottingham when Mark called. "Don't walk home by yourself tonight. I'll be there."

"You're always here," she laughed. "You didn't have to call to tell me that."

"I know. I guess I just wanted to hear you."

"Is everything OK?"

"Yeah." He sounded beat. "You just can't be too careful."

"Have you thought anymore about—?"

"Babies? Little else."

"I don't mind waiting," she said. "I want it to be the right time for you too."

After putting on his running shorts, Mark did his couple of miles on the Burke Gilman Trail, turning left where Mary had turned right, pounding toward the University Medical Center and Husky Stadium, hoping if he sweated enough, the smell that clung to his mind would be washed away.

Back in the apartment he took the hottest bath he could stand, brushed his teeth twice, flossed twice, and gargled. He didn't want to be in the apartment alone, so he went to Costa's for dinner and ate stuffed grape leaves and couscous. Then he went to the Seven Gables and saw Philip Noiret in *The Clockmaker*. At 9:30, he decided he needed a drink and walked to the Nottingham.

Mark entered through the lobby and saw Mary, but she was talking to a man at the front desk, and she didn't see him. Just as well. He passed through the restaurant and entered the bar. A band played "Proud Mary." Mark ordered a scotch and sipped it. The room was crowded. Women wearing stiletto heels danced and laughed. Their tanned shoulders, pristine and glorious, articulated with the straps of their sundresses. The whole fabulous structure of necks and shoulders, ridges and hollows, undid him.

He liked the little space that sometimes developed between shoulder and breast, which the strap bridged but didn't touch. In the winter, those shoulders would be white and cool as skinless apples. Oh, that these women could always be so fine, so firm and soft, and so essentially mysterious—that they could keep their mystery, and go to their graves in old age with peace, maybe even joy, having loved and been loved in return.

During the previous summer, in the months before the wedding, he had worked on the Olinski farm, sharing a bedroom with Mary's brother Fred. Mark had become very fond of the Olinskis. One of the things he loved was their directness. They did not defer doing what they wanted. Sure, they were cautious about money; with the ups and downs of farming, they had to be. But the Olinskis didn't conceive of themselves as works in progress. They were who they were and so could turn their attention to the rest of the world and what needed to be done.

The people Mark knew in Seattle, it seemed, had been born with master plans and were desperate about completing them— desperate about their unfinished states as human beings, always only halfway there. When, if ever, would these people have children? In their midthirties after making partner? After their spouses had also established their careers: M.A.s, Ph.Ds., tenure-track jobs, publication, tenure, more partnerships? How many would just put the kids off forever because they were too busy sculpting themselves?

The hardest work Mark had done that summer on the Olinski farm was baling hay. He'd stood on the jiggling wagon behind the hay baler while the tractor, like a little train engine, pulled both. The tractor rumbled along the rows of new-mown hay, and the baler scooped the hay off the ground and spit it back toward the man on the wagon in a nice compact rectangular block, bound with twine. The man on the wagon grabbed the bales as they came out of the baler and stacked them.

The challenge was balance. The wagon bumped and lurched along in the field, and Mark always felt in danger of falling off headfirst. At the end of the day, the muscles in his legs, hips, and abdomen quivered. Chaff from the hay invaded every crack and orifice of his body. The yellow dust had the power to penetrate clothing. Stalks of hay, sticking jagged-edged out of the bales, slashed at his forearms and left them a network of scratches.

One afternoon Mark broke the farm record by putting 132 bales on the wagon, and then 3 more for good measure. His shirt was plastered to his body with sweat, and his jeans were soaked around the belt. As he finished the load and some suspicious clouds darkened the west, Mary's brother Fred, on a second tractor, pulled an empty wagon out to the field, to exchange for the full one. Mary rode the empty wagon, carrying two thermos jugs of ice water. She handed one to her father and another to Mark.

"My turn to bale for a while," she said.

"Really?" Mark said.

Mr. Olinski laughed. "Take a break," he told Mark.

An apple tree stood in the middle of the field. Mark had given up on wearing glasses for the week because the lenses became encrusted with salt so fast. He sat against the apple tree, rubbed his aching back against the trunk, and watched the slightly blurred image of his wife-to-be deftly taking the bales and swinging them into position on the wagon. She didn't lurch, jerk, or stagger like he did. She never hugged the bale to keep from falling overboard. Her movements were smooth, balanced, economical. She used the bale to establish a center of gravity, out in space, around which she and the bale revolved. She turned one way, the bale turned another, and she dropped it into place. As the pile got higher, instead of stacking, back bent, she launched the bales with a powerful grace that involved her whole body, the energy traveling from legs, to shoulders, to arms, to a long, extended wrist, like a basketball player making a jump shot. The bales infallibly landed where she wanted. The tractor circled closer and closer to the apple tree, and Mark imagined the muscles in Mary's back going hard and soft as she launched each bale higher onto the wagon stack and swiveled to get the next. Her hair was in a long braid that whipped around as she worked.

He knew he had none of her grace or balance. He'd headbutted some of those last bales into place. His style was to abandon self and charge, until either he or the obstacle before him cracked and crumbled.

And now he was in a bar that was clouded with pheromones, a sexual riptide of human beings, and he knew that married or not, children or not, he would feel that tug for the rest of his life. Mary was right about having children: it was the last marriage vow, the one Paula Pierson was glad she hadn't made.

At 11:00, after his third scotch, Mark left the bar to get Mary. "I missed you," he said as they walked home. He stopped on Forty-fifth, over the freeway, and kissed her. Streams of red taillights shot toward Seattle.

"I missed you too," she said, and kissed him back. "Did you stop at the bar?"

"Yeah."

"Are you OK?"

"Sure."

"What did you do today?"

"Traffic cases. You know," he shrugged. "The usual. How about you?"

"I saw a dog get hit by a car."

"No!"

She told him.

"You carried it all the way from Northlake?"

"Yes."

He could just see her: "You want to ship him home?"

"Yes. If we can't find who he belongs to. Do you mind?"

"Hell, no. Save the dog."

"By the time we get done paying the vet, getting a crate to ship him in, I don't know, it might cost us a couple hundred bucks. At least."

"I don't care. I don't want anything dying around here."

They walked arm in arm back to La Paz. Mary leaned her head on his shoulder, sometimes, and told him the rest, how she had sold three-quarters of their paperbacks for $73.50, dropped out of graduate school, and tossed her birth control pills.

At the apartment, they brushed their teeth and washed their hands. He pushed the furniture against the wall, and she lowered the Murphy bed. The room seemed bigger to Mark without so many books. He picked up the Dürer print from where Mary had placed it against the wall. Behind the shattered glass was a mounted knight, erect in the saddle, a spear in his hand. A half-starved, craven-looking dog walked underneath his horse. Accompanying the knight was a fantastic-looking Satan, horns, ugly teeth, more goat than demon, and with him, Death, holding an hourglass. The knight seemed oblivious to his companions. Were they invisible? Had he grown so used to them he no longer paid attention?

Mary undressed. Mark undressed. For a moment, they stood naked, looking at each other, and then Mary lifted her arms and a sheath of cotton nightgown rippled over her.

"Are you too tired?" he asked. "To be gotten with child?"

"No," she said softly.

She raised her arms, and he slipped the nightgown over her as easily as it had fallen, running his hands along her sides and arms and hands. Their bodies touched, and he saw the scratches on her shoulder. Some ran from shoulder to elbow.

"Blackberry bushes," she said.

He kissed her shoulder gently, as if kissing it would make the cuts go away, as if he could keep her alive forever.

LITTLE ROUND TOP

It was our seventeenth anniversary, and I was late for dinner. The sun cut through the tinted glass of my old Civic, and the air conditioner, at full blast, did little more than dry sweat to my face. I had a bouquet of roses for Margo next to me on the passenger's seat; my head throbbed from inhaling cleaning chemicals all day, and I was waiting for a Hispanic woman with two kids to cross the street. I crept forward a little, my car angled for the right turn, when the guy behind me started to pound on his horn. I glanced at his reflection in the rearview mirror. He was a big guy with a fat face and black five o'clock shadow. His jaw moved up and down as he yelled, though I couldn't hear him. The woman had one kid on each side, their hands in hers, and she kept stepping into the street and then back onto the curb, looking around as if she and her kids had just materialized. Finally, she decided to make her move, and they started across the street, the kids pulling in various directions, as the pedestrian light began to blink "Wait." I looked at the roses and hoped they wouldn't wilt.

That's when the guy behind me just bore down on his horn. I thought: *Look at the crosswalk, asshole. What am I supposed to do? Run them over?* The woman gave me a dirty look over her shoulder. No doubt she thought it was me on the horn. The guy in back was now bouncing in his seat. He was in a Mercedes, a big black box of a car. He saw me looking at him, sat bolt upright, and met my eyes in the rearview mirror. He clenched his teeth, and as I

40

watched his eyes narrow, he rear-ended me hard enough to snap my seat belt tight. I switched off the ignition, shifted into first, and yanked up on the parking brake. Then I got out.

I looked at my rear bumper. No dents, but a little smudge and a scratch.

I walked slowly to the driver's side door of the Mercedes. Sun sprayed off the black car in long, thin needles. The jowly man inside was livid, wrestling back and forth, trying to disentangle his arm from his seat belt. As he struggled, the Mercedes rocked from side to side. I could see the door was going to open fast, so I stepped back. When the door sprang, the guy rose up at me like an animal out of a pit. He had greasy hair, a navy blue suit, and big meaty hands. I could see he was coming for me, but his girth hindered him, and his knees strained. Before he got upright, I took a step forward and jabbed him, short but hard, just beneath the spot where the ribs come together at the chest. His face looked like the man in the moon. He started to sink, and I hit him again, in the face, and again, and maybe a few more times. He collapsed to the pavement, wedged between the car door and the frame, and I thought, *Good God.* I'd felt the bridge of his nose crunch.

Blood flowed from his nose over his chin and onto his white shirt. The red stripes in his tie seemed to glow in response. He kept blinking and rolling his eyes, as if trying to focus. I wanted to help him get up, but I was afraid he'd punch me. After watching him blink a few more times, I decided to try anyway. I couldn't get at his hands, so I crouched down, got him in an awkward bear hug, and tried to stand. I couldn't get him back into his car. I couldn't even get him up. He just fell through my arms. There was no shape to him, nothing to grab. I tried to loosen his tie and got some blood on my hands. I had blood on my shirt from trying to lift him up.

"What did you do?" a woman asked, her hand going over her mouth. Cars were trying to get around us, people were walking over from Starbucks and the florist shop. Now the blood spread over his tie and jacket. He breathed heavily and stared at me, cringing. Heat rose in waves from the pavement, and I thought of his buttocks and thighs, frying on the concrete like spam.

"Are you all right?" I asked, squeaking like a thirteen-year-old.

"What happened?" somebody said.

"I was defending myself," I said. "The guy went crazy."

A Starbucks waitress was looking at me with big eyes. I go in there a lot.

"He just came at me," I said.

She didn't say a word.

"He swung first," I said, feeling myself flush from the lie.

"Here, let me help you," I told the man. I tried again to get some purchase under his arms and raise him up. He went limp. His armpits were squishy, and I couldn't budge him.

Eventually the cops got there. And an ambulance.

"I was just defending myself," I told the cop who questioned me.

"I don't know if we're going to charge you with anything," he said, "but if I was you, I think I'd call my lawyer."

But I don't have a lawyer, I wanted to tell him. Not like I have a doctor or dentist. Most people just don't *have* lawyers. Who wants them?

I was way late to take Margo for dinner. After I pulled into the garage and turned the ignition, I lay my head on the steering wheel, and for a fierce moment struggled to hold back tears. I looked down at the mess on my shirt, picked up the roses, and went inside. Margo and the kids were sitting at the kitchen table, no doubt wondering where on earth I'd been. I could tell Margo was miffed, until she really saw me.

"Jack, what happened? Are you all right?" She jumped out of her chair, afraid to touch me before she knew the damage. After telling her the blood on the shirt was not mine, I took my shirt off and sat down.

"What happened! what happened!" the kids both kept yelling, and though it was the last thing I wanted to do, I started talking once again, forced to make the whole mess come alive. Margo got me a glass of water. They all listened, bug-eyed. "He just erupted out of the car." I said. "A big black Mercedes. He swung first, so I had to hit him. He was a big guy. Must have outweighed me by a hundred pounds."

Margo gave me a hug and looked sympathetic, her fine, blue eyes tearing up. "Thank God he didn't hurt you," she said.

We decided not to go out. Margo made bacon and eggs. I couldn't eat, so I went downstairs to my shop. The familiar squeak of the stairs was comforting. Last summer, I painted the cinder-block walls of the basement in a high-gloss off-white, so the lighting would be better. The washer and drier were down there and a big table that held my simulation of the battle of Gettysburg, late the second day, when John Bell Hood attacked the Devil's Den and Little Round Top.

I had a long workbench against one wall. I kept it neat. On it were several small jars of paint. The bench itself was stained with the spatters of various colors, greens and browns, and any color that might be found on a flag or the uniform of a Civil War soldier. Paintbrushes, bristles up, filled two quart jars. I'd trimmed some of the brushes so only a few bristles remained, and I used them for the finest detail work. To the right of my chair, I had a big magnifying glass, attached to an arm that swiveled and bent like an elbow, the kind of magnifier that jewelers use. I also had magnifiers that fit on my eyeglasses. I did a lot of things at the workbench. I constructed Little Round Top there, and the boulders of the Devil's Den. For a previous scenario, I had built the bridge at Antietam.

Margo had told me more than once that I was still just a kid who liked to color, except that instead of trying to stay inside the lines of a drawing, I colored little lead soldiers that I bought a few at a time, three or four times a year, at a store in Cambria. Doing this detail work, as slowly as I pleased, was the most relaxing thing in my life. A hundred years ago I might have been some kind of artisan, working on things like cuckoo clocks. But to earn a living I cleaned carpets, as fast as I could, trying to get as much work crammed into a day as possible, while keeping an eye on my employees to make sure they did the same. Carpet cleaners still droned in my head at lunch and dinner, but when I was in the basement, I didn't hear them anymore.

My right hand hurt so much it was hard to hold a brush. But after an hour or so by myself, finishing work on two Confederate soldiers, the image of the man I had struck and the blood pouring out of his nose was well enough contained that I could go back upstairs. I watched a *Star Trek* rerun with the kids, and we all had some ice cream to celebrate the day. Later, as I watched myself in the bathroom mirror, brushing my teeth, I thought about hitting the man in the body, and how it had felt like punching into a jelly donut.

I took Margo out to dinner the next evening, to make up for the missed date. We went to Giulia's, an Italian restaurant that's normally way out of our price range. We save it for special occasions. I love the place. Waiters in tuxedos wait on you as if your comfort is the most important thing on earth. Frank Sinatra or Dean Martin croons, or somebody like Pavarotti sings opera. Glasses clink cheerfully behind the bar. It all helped to mask the clanking inside my head, the face that sometimes got past lock and key to present itself in a bloody stupor.

Wine came. The waiter poured a swallow into my glass, and I tasted it, feeling silly. "It's just fine," I told him. As he left, Margo and I giggled, thinking the same thought: *as if* we'd *know*. We sipped wine and ate bread.

A lot of women wear their hair short when they get to Margo's age, but she's always kept her hair long. It used to be crow-feather black, but now it has picked up a lot of gray. She's never dyed it and doesn't intend to.

"You're worried about yesterday, aren't you?" Margo said.

I shrugged.

"Do you think you're going to get in trouble?"

"Well, I did give the guy a bloody nose."

"But you talked to the police."

"Yes."

"And they didn't do anything?"

"No. But . . . You never can tell what people will do. I just don't understand it. I haven't been in a fight since eighth grade. Why did I have to hit him?"

"But you didn't have any choice. He tried to hit you first."

I rolled my glass, watching the wine swirl. My hand still ached from the day before. I should tell her now, I thought. The whole thing. She'll understand. She'll even feel more sympathetic. We'll go home, make love after the kids get tucked away. We'll be in this together.

"But I still feel bad," I said.

She reached across the table and put her hand on mine.

"I'm sorry," I said.

"For what?"

"Complicating things."

She smiled in a way that said I was being ridiculous. "Don't worry. Let's try to forget it for tonight. It's our anniversary. And I love you."

Talk about luck. It turned out the guy I had hit was a lawyer. Within two days, I was served a summons and complaint for a civil suit. Assault and battery. Medical bills. Pain and suffering. He was suing me for exactly one million dollars. Soon after that I was informed by the Fresno County District Attorney that criminal charges were being filed against me and that I would have to appear in court to be arraigned.

A month later my lawyer, Bill Salerno—by then I could say "my lawyer" as if he were a relative—showed me a picture of the guy's face, taken a few days after I'd hit him. His name was Clark Kinderman. He looked out at me from the picture. Bandages criss-crossed the bridge of his nose. His eyes, red slits, glared out of swollen, black-and-blue flesh. "Jesus," I said. "He didn't look that bad." Had I done this?

"You've got one big problem," Salerno told me. "You obviously hit him more than once. Even if we convince a jury that he came after you first, you can only use reasonable force to fend off an attack. I got this picture from the prosecuting attorney. You can bet it's going to come up in the civil suit too. Why did you just keep hitting him?"

I shook my head.

"Were you afraid he'd get back up and attack you?"

I nodded. "Yeah. That's it."

"I'm trying to put this criminal trial off as long as possible, so the jury doesn't get to see him until he's healed completely. Given the way court calendars are backed up, that won't be hard."

"Do you think they'll put me in jail?"

"What you've got going for you is that your record is Jesus-clean, and nobody really saw what happened in the fight, but the man behind Kinderman did see him hit your car. He saw your car bounce, which gives you an excuse for approaching Kinderman. It's just your word against Kinderman's as to who threw the first punch, and I think it's very unlikely that a jury will think, beyond a reasonable doubt, that a guy your size started a fight with someone as big as Kinderman. Lastly, Kinderman is a notoriously hot-tempered son-of-a-bitch. Judges don't like him. Juries don't like him. Even the deputy prosecutor doesn't like him. I think the prosecutor is halfway ready to drop the case as it is."

Sure enough, a few weeks later Salerno called to tell me the criminal charges had been dropped. "Now all we have to get ready for is the civil trial," Salerno said. "And that's over a year away."

"I like it when you iron down here," I told Margo one night. "I like the smell of the iron on the clothes and your steady back-and-forth rhythm—the hiss of the steam."

She raised her eyebrows as if to say, *Give me a break,* but I could tell she liked it.

The house was very quiet. I daubed some brown on a Confederate soldier's belt. "We're here, doing two different things, but we're really together, like we've grown invisible nerves into each other. Sometimes, during the day, when I'm cleaning a carpet, I think I can feel you. I can sense when you want to talk to me."

"Yes." She smiled. "So can I."

I wasn't quite telling the truth. I hadn't felt that link to Margo since the fight. There was too much interference in my head. Too much Kinderman. Or maybe I'd broken the link by not telling Margo what had really happened. I remembered the night of our anniversary dinner, wishing I had told her then, and I thought, *why not now, while she's ironing and I'm painting, and everything is so normal?* But I'd kept hitting Kinderman. I'd hit him again and again.

"Christian Couples tomorrow," Margo said, as the iron thumped against the board.

"Right."

"Maybe we should just skip," she said.

"Why?"

"I don't know," she said. "I just feel like a little break."

I was surprised. We went to Northwest Church every Sunday, and we went to Christian Couples every other Wednesday night. Margo had had to drag me to the first meeting of CC. I thought it would be like some encounter group where everyone spilled their guts about their marriages as if they were on a Baptist version of Ricki Lake. But it wasn't like that. We all believed that if we put God first in our lives, our marriages and family lives would prosper.

It had worked for Margo and me. We had only three years of community college between us, but we'd come a long way. At the first of every month Margo and I paid the bills together. We went through the credit card purchases. If the checkbook didn't balance, she would work on it until it did. She did the books for my business and gave me advice. In fact, she had talked me into starting the business, and now I had seven industrial contracts and four men working for me. We'd had no secrets from each other, financial or otherwise, and no secrets from anyone else either. How clean and sweet it had been to live so open to inspection.

When I had gone to court with Salerno to plead "not guilty" to the criminal charges, of course Margo had come with me. After the arraignment, as we'd walked across the courthouse lawn, she had said, "Maybe it would be better not to mention any of this at Christian Couples." I had just nodded my head.

"It's hard to explain."

I nodded again.

"I think we can get through this by ourselves, and with God's help."

"Yes," I'd said. "That ought to be enough."

The iron gave off a burst of steam. I dipped a clean brush with only a few bristles into a jar of brass-colored paint and applied it to the buttons of a Union soldier. Margo rearranged a shirt on the ironing board.

"You're sure you don't want to go?" I asked, peering at my work through the magnifying glass.

"Yes. I'm a little worn-out this week."

"I love you."

"I love you too," she said, going after a wrinkle.

Sometimes I saw what had happened as my fault, and I wished I were Catholic, so I could go to at least one human being and confess. I found out it was a lot easier to say "forgive us our trespasses" when I didn't think I had any trespasses worth mentioning. I prayed for forgiveness, and I prayed for help too, because the main emotion I felt was fear. At the same time, I had no faith in my prayers. I couldn't sleep through the night. What if Kinderman got a huge judgment? One million dollars. Fear made me see the "accident," as I had started to think of it, as a kind of natural disaster, or some dark thing that God had designed for me as a test. If only I hadn't been at that intersection at that specific time. If only that lady with the kids hadn't been there, or had just crossed the street as soon as the light turned. If only the guy behind me hadn't been such a shit. I had a list of "if-onlys" that went on all night.

I couldn't eat. Normally, I come home hungry, but food wasn't food. I'd catch the kids looking at me, worried. I couldn't concentrate to help them with their homework. Things that never used to bother me—toys left strewn around, dirty socks on the floor, the messes that kids make all the time—got on my nerves unbearably. I yelled at the kids. I had fights with Margo. I grew listless about building up my business, which before the accident had just begun to take off.

"Jesus. What if he bankrupts us," I'd mutter at various times throughout the day.

Margo hadn't seemed too concerned, didn't even seem to think it was real, until we met with Salerno, and we started talking about possible damages. She hadn't had a job in years and didn't want to go back to work. She wanted to help me build the business and to be there for the kids when they came home from school. Down the road, she wanted a new house, and our first son was only five years from college. We were worth about a hundred thousand bucks, including home equity, and that had come hard. I didn't work for the state. I had to pay for my own retirement and my family's health insurance.

"What if he gets it all?" I said one night.

Margo screamed at me. "Can't you ever stop thinking about this? Can't you stop *dwelling* on it?"

"OK, OK."

"I am so sick of listening to you talk about nothing else. What am I supposed to do?"

"Nothing," I mumbled.

"It's making you sick. It's making *me* sick."

"I'm sorry. I won't mention it anymore."

"How can he collect a million dollars for a little punch in the nose? How can he get anything? For God's sake, just relax. . . ." It took a lot to get Margo riled, but when she got on a roll, it was just as hard to get her off.

After that I thought it would be best if I quarantined myself, and I spent a lot more time in the basement working on Little Round Top. There was much to do. I forested my papier-mâché hills with little trees made of twigs and green sponge. I kept the trees relatively sparse. I wanted to suggest a dense forest, but I wanted the soldiers to be clearly visible. I had a few Union soldiers in place, a suggestion of the Twentieth Maine, commanded by Colonel Joshua Chamberlain, and I had a few Confederate soldiers, of the Fifteenth Alabama, coming up the hill. I was wondering where to place Strong Vincent, the twenty-six-year-old Union colonel from Harvard who had seen the importance of Little Round Top, fortified it, and in so doing, probably saved the Union.

Two things had gotten me interested in Little Round Top. First, there was the Ted Turner movie *Gettysburg*. Then there was the vacation we'd taken the previous summer to Gettysburg and Washington, D. C. We'd spent two days exploring the battlefield, and the kids had climbed all over the Devil's Den. Even Margo, who had been dubious about the Gettysburg trip, had found herself absorbed in stories of soldiers and citizens caught in the battle. A park ranger got me interested in digging deeper into what happened at Little Round Top. I read books on it and actual reports by officers who had been in the battle.

In the movie, Joshua Chamberlain, who was on the extreme left flank of the Union army, saved the day by holding onto Little Round Top, withstanding charge after charge from the rebel army. Finally, with his men nearly out of ammunition, Chamberlain gathered his officers together and gave directions for a bayonet charge that would have the Twentieth Maine pivoting like a door on a hinge, from left to right. It was either attack or retreat, and retreat was unthinkable, because if the left flank gave way, the entire Union line would collapse, and if the line collapsed, Robert E. Lee's Army of Northern Virginia would march into Washington, D. C. At the crest of the rebel attack, Chamberlain gave the signal, and his men swung in a line, those on the far left wheeling right. The men of the Twentieth Maine swept the Confederate attackers before them, and at the bottom of the hill, captured many of the survivors.

In Chamberlain's actual report, however, there was no mention of a conference with officers, and no indication of the door-hinge maneuver. Chamberlain wrote that in the midst of battle, he yelled, "Fix bayonets," and the order "ran like fire along the line from man to man, and rose into a shout, with which they sprang forward upon the enemy, now not thirty yards away." The Southern attack broke in the face of the bayonet charge. Confusion was so great that a Confederate officer fired his pistol without effect into the face of a Union officer while simultaneously offering him his sword.

Colonel William C. Oates, who commanded the attacking Confederate troops, the Fifteenth Alabama, disagreed with Chamberlain about what had happened at Little Round Top. Oates's men had marched for sixteen hours the day before their assault, just to reach Gettysburg. On the day of their attack, they then marched the entire length of the battlefield, north to south, a distance of about five miles. They were ordered to attack Big Round Top, a hill to the south of Little Round Top, and they captured it, making a long, steep climb, through heavy brush and boulders, under fire from Union snipers. Exhausted, reeling from dehydration, they were then ordered to capture Little Round Top, which they attempted to do time after time, still absorbing fire from behind by snipers left on Big Round Top. Finally, his men utterly spent, Oates ordered a retreat. It was during the retreat, Oates maintained, that Chamberlain's men made their charge. And here, I wonder about Chamberlain's account. His men certainly attacked. Did he exaggerate the strength of that last Confederate attack? Did his regiment actually fix bayonets?

Is embellishment required when translating the experience of battle to those who've never had it?

What I had not told Margo grew between us like a scarred membrane. At a meeting with Margo and me, Salerno mentioned, in passing, that he'd received some more pictures from Kinderman's attorney. Salerno was digging them out of his file but made eye contact with me and changed the subject. Margo saw what passed between us. She wasn't one to miss anything.

"You don't want her to see the pictures," Salerno said the next day, over the phone.

"No."

"As far as she knows, this was just a little fight."

"Yeah."

"No real damage."

"Nope."

"You know this is all going to come out at trial. You'd better talk to her."

"Yeah." *Maybe she won't go to the trial,* I thought.

As if reading my mind, Salerno said, "I'm going to want her at the trial. Supporting her husband. And I don't want her to react to anything."

"OK."

"Maybe you should get some counseling," Salerno said.

"You're my counselor. My lawyer."

"Then tell her."

We lay in bed, staring at the ceiling. Once, sex had been an important part of our lives, but now, we couldn't find comfort in it. Instead we relied on speech, as if we could talk the poison out of ourselves.

Margo said, "It's just not fair. Why should you have to pay anything? You were just defending yourself. You were just sitting there and he ran into your car on purpose. Why should we have to suffer for what a horrible man like that does?"

"Well," I said, "there's what happened, and there's what looks like what happened when you get to court."

"Who can tell the best story," she said.

"Maybe. But we've got witnesses."

"I don't suppose those pictures Bill Salerno mentioned will help."

"No," I said, wanting to lose myself in her long dark hair.

She rolled toward me and looked into the side of my face: "What did they look like?"

"Oh, not much. Just a few pictures Kinderman had taken of himself after I hit him."

"So? What did they look like?"

"He looked a little messed up."

"How messed up?"

"I broke his nose. You know that. He didn't look all that good."

"Jack, have you told me everything?"

"I defended myself."

Margo propped herself on one elbow. "Did he really try to hit you first?"

"Maybe I hit him first. Everything happened fast."

"Surely you've got to know."

"I guess I was scared. Maybe I hit him in kind of an automatic reaction. I mean, the guy rammed me."

"You don't know whether you hit him first?"

I sat up. "You've lived with me for seventeen years. Do you think I *would* hit him first? What are you, his goddamn lawyer?"

She was silent for a while. "I'm sorry. I'm sure it was awful."

"You sound like you think I'm some kind of thug."

"Jack, no."

"What happened is hard to describe."

"Why don't you try? Just keep trying until it's all out. You think I don't know it's eating on you all the time? It wouldn't be if you got it all out."

"Why couldn't I just have been somewhere else? Some other florist. Or why couldn't I have been there five minutes earlier? Or later?"

I couldn't sleep. I went downstairs in the middle of the night, gazed at the battlefield, and thought of Chamberlain. Before the war, he had been a minister and then a professor of rhetoric and the Bible at Bowdoin College. He was wounded six times during the war, and nearly died from a bullet wound at Petersburg. Rising to the rank of major general, he received the surrender of weapons from the Army of Northern Virginia at Appomattox. I wondered if all of the bloodshed that had engulfed him from Fredericksburg to Appomattox bothered his conscience. I wondered what his prayers had been like, if he'd ever found it hard to pray.

I knew there were certain things we'd be able to keep, even if we declared bankruptcy, but I didn't know exactly what. Salerno did not clarify this for me. He kept saying, "It's too early to think about that. And I'm not going to let that happen. After all, I want to get paid too." Then he'd chuckle. He never used the word *bankruptcy*. I kept thinking of movers invading my house and cleaning it out, taking Little Round Top, table and all.

"If you want something," I told Margo, "just go ahead and buy it." Of course, she didn't.

I took more time off. The thought that I might be cleaning carpet after carpet to pay Kinderman made me sick. One day I drove to Cambria and spent five hundred dollars on lead Civil War soldiers and paint. A few weeks later I got the urge to paint cannon and went to Cambria again. I didn't tell Margo. I paid cash so she wouldn't see it in the checkbook or on the credit card. I stashed the soldiers in a footlocker under my workbench and just let them appear as I painted them, assembly-line style, in platoons and squads.

Nightly I filched lead soldiers from the footlocker, and coated them with blue and gray. Before, I had always painted one soldier at a time, in no hurry to complete them, but now I was going at it the same way I cleaned carpets. Each night I worked on four groups of soldiers at the same time. There was the group I overcoated with blue and gray, and another group, blue and gray from the previous evening, on which I painted the larger details of belts, sashes, backpacks, guns, and swords. To the third and fourth groups, on which the second level of detail had dried, I added the finest painting: flesh, variations in uniform color, buttons, insignia, braid, some facial features. One night, looking at the soldiers on the workbench, the artillery pieces pointed in my direction, it seemed as if I was under attack, the target of a temporary Union-Confederate alliance.

We offered Kinderman ten thousand dollars, all of our ready cash. He refused to settle. Salerno said, "I talked to Kinderman's lawyer, but Kinderman demanded to speak to me directly. He told me he wants revenge. He wants to make you suffer. And he wants you to know that."

By the day of the civil trial, over a year after the criminal case had been dismissed, I had lost more than thirty pounds. I looked scrawny. If anything, Kinderman had gained weight. Instead of filling his suit, he bulged in it. This was all to the good, Salerno said: "He looks like he could snap you in two." Kinderman hulked next to his lawyer at the counsel table. His shaved cheeks were dark with the roots of his beard, and his eyes were like black glass. Salerno had told me to wear Dockers, a shirt and a tie, but no jacket. Margo sat as the only spectator in the courtroom, directly behind me. Salerno had wanted the kids there as well, but I'd refused.

The civil trial was over in a day. The morning was spent picking the jury, which looked like a sample of the people who attended my own church, maybe one pew's worth. The judge seemed neither bored nor interested. This trial was not going to be the high point of his week. Lunch was a quiet affair between Margo and me. She put her hand on mine as we spooned courthouse chili.

Court reconvened at 2:00. Salerno gave me a big smile and a thump on the back. "Now we'll take it to 'em."

Kinderman was the first person to testify. His lawyer was short, thin, and sandy-haired, the opposite of Kinderman, and he asked questions in an intent monotone. He gave the impression that an answer to any question he asked Kinderman would have to be the truth—for how else could you answer a computer?

Kinderman testified that he was a personal injury lawyer. He was leaving the shopping center at Shaw and Feland, where he'd stopped to buy a cell phone at the Pacific Bell store. He was behind me, waiting to make a right-hand turn, and I wasn't moving with the green light, so he tapped his horn.

"Was anyone in the crosswalk, going across Shaw Avenue?" his lawyer asked.

"No."

"Did Mr. Boyer move when you honked your horn?"

"No." Kinderman shifted around on the witness stand, as if he was trapped.

"Then what happened?"

"My car's idle speed was too high at the time, and if I took my foot off the brake, the car would shoot forward. My foot slipped when I was shifting in my seat, and I hit the car in front of me."

"Mr. Boyer's car?"

"Yes."

"What did the defendant do?"

"Boyer got out of his car," Kinderman said, "checked his rear bumper, which was fine—I barely tapped it—and then he came to my door. I was getting out to apologize, and he just hit me in the solar plexus. I didn't get to say a word. I have stomach trouble, and the pain was excruciating. It took my breath away, and as I slumped to the ground, he hit me in the face, time after time. He was like a madman."

"Objection," Salerno said.

"Sustained," said the judge.

"What kind of stomach trouble do you have?" Kinderman's lawyer asked.

"Duodenal ulcers."

Kinderman glared at me, clenching and unclenching his fists, which he had propped on the witness stand. His jaw tightened, and his eyes bulged.

I whispered to Salerno: "He looked the same way when he came after me."

"Good," Salerno wrote on a legal pad.

"Did you ever try to strike Mr. Boyer?" the lawyer asked.

"No."

"Did you even attempt to defend yourself?"

"I couldn't. He knocked the wind out of me with his first punch."

"What happened then?"

"He got me in a kind of bear hug, and started banging me back and forth between the car and the door."

"Did you defend yourself?"

"I thought my best chance was to just play dead."

The jury tittered.

Kinderman's lawyer then set up an easel in front of the jury, and put a blowup of Kinderman's face on it. The picture showed Kinderman before he'd been treated for the broken nose. Somehow, he'd gotten a camera even before the emergency room doctor had gone to work. His long nose lay flabbily toward one side of his face. The swelling had already started. There was still blood on his chin, over his shirt and tie. I heard Margo's intake of breath behind me. During the whole time Kinderman had testified, I had felt Margo's gaze on the back of my neck.

The next blowup was the one I had seen before, Kinderman the next day, with his red-slitted eyes, purple flesh, and bandaged nose. The next two were left and right views, and what followed was a nightmare of testimony about trouble breathing, deviated septums, possible future surgery, and recurrent nightmares about being beaten by me. The jury wasn't laughing now.

The rest of the trial was a blur to me, even my own testimony. Salerno put a doctor on the stand to say that Kinderman, essentially, had received a bloody nose, which had indeed been broken, but was now fully healed. The doctor said Kinderman's septum was just fine, and that no future surgery would be required. Other witnesses took the stand and testified to what little they'd seen and heard.

"He tried to help the man back into his car," one lady said. "Hit his car with a good jolt," another man said, "I saw it bounce." Another witness said, "The man in the Mercedes was honking his horn constantly."

I snuck glances at Kinderman during all of this. His jaw worked back and forth like a mastiff's chewing on a bone, just the way he'd looked in my rearview mirror.

At last, I took the witness stand. The microphone coiled in my face. I put my hand on the Bible and swore to tell the whole truth and nothing but the truth, so help me God. I testified that it was my anniversary, and I just wanted to get home to be with my family. I talked a lot about my family. This was what Salerno had called, "playing the family angle." The jury, he said, wouldn't believe that a man on the day of his anniversary would take time to start a fistfight with someone twice his size. I talked about my carpet-cleaning business and how Margo had helped me build it up. This, Salerno said, was "the class angle," showing a fat cat lawyer beating up on a small-time, blue-collar, working man. I talked about my church. Salerno never said this was the religious angle, but I suppose it was. I testified about the woman with the kids and Kinderman laying on the horn. I testified that Kinderman came out of the car like an enraged bull, and I admitted to hitting him more than once in the face: "I was afraid he was going to get up and kill me," I said. When Kinderman took the stand for the second time, he said, "I was afraid he *was* killing me."

After the jury went out to deliberate, and the judge retired to chambers, Salerno whispered to me, "Kinderman was our best witness. Did you get a load of that body language? He wanted to take you apart right here. How did you like my closing argument?"

"It was great," I said, even though I couldn't remember a word.

Chairs scraped, and Kinderman passed behind us, leaving the courtroom with his lawyer.

"Our biggest problem," Salerno said, not bothering to keep the admiration out of his voice, "is that you really creamed the guy."

I turned to look at Margo, who no longer seemed to recognize me. "Can we leave?" she asked Salerno.

"It's up to you. It's not a criminal trial, so you don't have to be here for the verdict. It's hard to say how long the jury will take."

"I want to go home," she said to me.

"What if the jury comes back?"

"I need to go."

"Just take the car," I said. "I'll get a cab."

I walked her to an elevator, and we went down to the courthouse garage in silence. "Are you all right?" I asked. She just took the keys from me and got into the car. I watched her until she disappeared around a corner.

A couple hours later the jury returned and awarded Kinderman five thousand dollars.

When I had been on the witness stand, it had seemed higher

than it looked, and when I got off, I had wobbled coming down the steps. Now, as Salerno and I walked away from the court-room, I still felt that wobble. Kinderman came out behind us and said to my back: "Hey Boyer? Who got in the last punch?"

I turned, none too steady, surprised at just how much I want-ed to hit him again.

Salerno grabbed my arm at the biceps: "Don't let him get to you. An award of five thousand dollars is nothing, and he knows it. Half of what we offered. This was a win." It struck me then that during the trial, of all the people in the courtroom, Kinderman had been the one I understood the best.

Margo had waited dinner for me. Spaghetti. I joked with the kids for the first time in months, and they laughed nervously, checking their mother. After, I went downstairs. Little Round Top was almost complete, the battleground packed with soldiers. "A cast of thousands," Margo had said, as the lead warriors magi-cally appeared. I thought it was time to start painting the three principles: Oates, Chamberlain, and Vincent. I wavered about who to paint first. It seemed an important decision. Vincent had died on Little Round Top, probably picked off by a sniper in the Devil's Den. Not for the first time, I wished I could sculpt a spe-cial figure, a real Strong Vincent, showing him the instant before he was shot, giving orders for the defense of the hill.

I had a lead figure that was obviously an officer. I put it under the magnifying glass. I could almost imagine an expression there. Was it desperation? Satisfaction? Who would it be? I dipped a thick brush into a bottle of Union blue and touched it to his cap. I had most of him blued in when I heard Margo's squeak on the stairs. She was behind my back, moving to the table.

"I can't get the pictures out of my head," she said.

"What pictures?" I asked stupidly.

"The pictures of *Kinderman*, Jack. Who else? What got into you?"

"I don't know."

"You've never told me the truth, have you? You just get this look on your face when you talk about it. Like you're not home. I've never seen it in you before."

I got up and walked to the battlefield table, next to Margo.

"OK. He didn't swing at me."

"Then you *lied*. You put your hand on the *Bible* and lied."

"I was protecting my family!"

"From what?"

"Financial disaster! Ruin! He lied. He lied half the time he was up there. What was I supposed to do? Assume the position?"

"Is that why you lied to *me*?"

"I didn't want to."

"But you did!" She was on the verge of tears, and I desperately did not want her to cry.

"Look. I don't know what happened that day. Did he actually make a motion with his arm to punch me? No. But was that punch going to come? Damn right it was. I could see it in his eyes. Or maybe he was just going to put his hands around my throat and squeeze. How do you explain that to somebody? 'I could see it in his eyes'? I told the truth in a way people would understand it."

"But why did you keep hitting him? My God, his face. . . ."

"I don't know. I have asked myself that question every day, hundreds of times a day, for the last year and a half. I can't remember how I felt. I can't remember feeling anything. I was angry when he was honking at me, seething when he hit my car. I was scared when his door flew open. But I can't remember how I felt when I was hitting him. Maybe I didn't feel anything."

"You've never talked to me about any of this." A tear rolled past the corner of her mouth.

"Some things aren't easy to talk *about*. Did you see him in court today? Do you think for a minute he didn't come after me?"

She looked at Little Round Top. "Where have all these soldiers come from?"

"From Cambria."

"You went to Cambria?"

"Yes."

"How much did you spend?"

"A lot. It helped me keep from going out of my mind."

"When?"

"I don't know. I don't even remember anymore."

"But why didn't you tell me?"

"I couldn't."

She waited for me to say something more, granite-faced despite the tears. Then she turned to go upstairs.

"Margo, maybe God takes into account more things than we do."

"That's convenient."

"It's what I hope."

After I heard the door at the top of the stairs close, I stood at the battle table and looked down. Above me, plates and glasses clinked. The dishwasher came on. Margo's footsteps groaned on the ceiling. Beneath me soldiers clashed on the south side of Little Round Top. I could almost feel myself down there with them, smoke hanging in the trees, acrid and dense as fog. Soft lead bullets and musket balls chewing up bark, leaves, trees, splattering off rock, and thunking into men's bodies and faces. I imagined the screaming of the wounded, the shouting of officers, the rebel yell echoing up the hill. Was it possible, under the conditions of battle, to have an order to fix bayonets "sweep down the line from man to man" until the wounded regiment got up with one mind and rushed to the attack? Or was every man, isolated in the smoke and noise, fighting his own battle against panic and the enemy? I gazed at the table, at each soldier that had taken hours to paint, at the lay of the terrain as I had made it with my hands, and the battle appeared.

Within thirty yards of Chamberlain's line, the Fifteenth Alabama is past what men can take. What's left of the regiment dies from bullets and stumbles from exhaustion. Some lean against trees, sucking air and praying they don't get shot. The attack begins to fall apart, and maybe Chamberlain, swinging his sword, yells, "Fix bayonets," or maybe an ordinary soldier starts down the hill, swinging an empty musket like a club. Maybe he is so scared he'd just as soon die and end his part of the battle then. Maybe

his fear has given way to rage. A few men follow. Some have bayonets fixed and some don't. Soon, the whole Twentieth Maine is
running downhill after a ragtag group of Confederate soldiers,
who are running whether they've heard an order or not. Nothing
has been planned. It has just happened. And all the testimony and
all the reports thereafter are so much paper, pasted to an event
only God can see.

ROUTE 18

I'm on Route 18 again, the only coast-to-coast one-way highway in the United States of America. Two lanes, but not a lot of traffic. It starts in New Jersey and ends in northern California. You can get off Route 18, onto gravel roads, or into little cities that have one or two gas stations, a motel, and a burger joint. But the roads that leave 18 always circle back, so there's really no getting off it. I don't know what's at the end. Maybe a parking lot the size of Rhode Island.

The dashed white line that divides Route 18 is pretty faded. In the daytime, it's just a lighter shade of gray than the road, obscured by tar and the marks of skidding tires. On a wet night, with your headlights splashing off oil and water, you can't even tell it's there.

Mainly, Route 18 is way out in the country. It doesn't cross any main roads but snakes its way under and over them in tunnels and bridges. It goes over the whole top of St. Louis, even the Freedom Arch—like a ribbon in the sky.

Sometimes I drive Route 18, at night, a thunderstorm off in the distance, and a small town ahead, with one seedy motel and a church nobody goes to anymore. A tattered old grain elevator leans against the stars. There's a diner where a few old, gristly men and a sleazy waitress listen to Johnny Cash on the jukebox. The stools at the counter are covered in cracked green vinyl patched with duct tape, and dirty ashtrays litter the counter and the tables. The old men joke and chuckle, phlegm rising in their throats. The smell of chicken potpie mixes with cigarette smoke. But now, it's a sunny morning on Route 18. Bright cotton clouds pile up on themselves, and winter wheat, just pushing up, sparkles green against the black soil. I could drive for hours. The top is down on my convertible, and the wind blows my hair straight back, like the tail of a comet. I'm sixteen, and I have a license to drive anywhere.

Dr. Singbat Grewal is a tall, chocolate-colored psychiatrist from India. Everything he says comes out like a question: "How nice to see you again?" I've been seeing him since seventh grade, when my mother saw a TV show about teen suicide and decided I was depressed. That was over three years ago. A big stack of files rests at his elbow, and he has just pulled mine off the top. He stares at my file with a puzzled expression, trying to remember who I am.

"So how are things going now . . . Linda?" he asks vaguely as his eyes soften to kind receptiveness. I can practically hear the screech of machinery as his pupils widen and the corners of his mouth go up.

"Oh, fine," I say.

"Hmmm," he says, groping. "Are you sleeping well?"

"Sometimes."

"Only sometimes?"

"I wake up around 2:00 or 3:00, and then I can't get back to sleep for a few hours. Sometimes." The possible side effects of Paxil (alias paroxetine) are nausea, drowsiness, sweating, tremor, a feeling of numbness, dizziness, dry mouth, and insomnia. I looked it up on the Internet. I don't think I have any of these, but the stuff makes me feel jumpy, which I think is different than having a tremor. When I started taking the stuff, Dr. Grewal told my mom and me that there were no side effects. So I tell him, "I feel jumpy. Sometimes I can't sleep."

"You need more exercise," he says, switching to a more imperative, Indian-father mode.

"I'm on the volleyball team. The marching band."

"You should run too. Running is good for you." When he says "good" it comes out like "geewd." He sounds like he's using his tongue to stir a batch of brownies. "It makes endorphins—these are the chemicals your body produces to make you feel good."

I know what endorphins are. And serotonin and all that stuff. He mentions them every time I come in. I've read about depression and panic attacks, which are what he thinks I've got. "Are you socializing with people more? Not hiding in your room?"

"Yes to both," I say.

He looks confused.

"Yes, I'm not hiding in my room." I couldn't hide in my room if I wanted to, since at Mom's I now have to share my room with my little half sister Eileen, and at Dad and Martha's I share it with my other little twin half sisters, Karen and Lori.

"How about boys? Are you interested in boys?"

"Not much," I say.

He nods his head, smiling. "Plenty of time for boys later. Now it is the time for you to study, so you can get into a good college. How is school work going?"

"All *A*'s," I say.

He beams at me, as if I could almost make the grade as an Indian daughter. "That is very good. We will raise your doses of Paxil from thirty to fifty milligrams a day, and see if that helps you to sleep." He goes into the waiting room to get my mother. When she comes in, he asks her the same questions he asked me, and she gives the same answers but doesn't say anything about how nervous I can get. Mom doesn't rat me out unless pressure is applied.

Mom and Dad have joint custody of me, so every two weeks I switch homes, enabling me to experience a broader range of dysfunctional family life. I'd like to escape, but my dad won't let me sleep over at my best friend's anymore. He says Kathy is a bad influence. My mother and Leonard won't let me do it either; when I ask, Mom gets this wounded expression on her face and says, "You spend so much time with your father. I get to see so little of you, I just want to keep you to myself when you're here." That doesn't stop her from going out with Leonard and leaving me with the two little kids to baby-sit. But when she and Leonard leave for the Outback Steakhouse and a movie, the first thing I do is call Kathy.

Kathy comes over and brings the latest issue of *Seventeen* with her. Dad won't let me get *Seventeen*. He says it's for sluts, which most high school girls are. Kathy says we're already too old for it, even though we're only sixteen, and she's right. The articles are pretty stupid, but we look at the advertisements and giggle.

This time they've got an article about kissing. Approach vectors. Synchronization. Contact. How long to hang in there. What can go wrong. The article should be called "Air Traffic Control." I haven't kissed a boy yet, even as an experiment, because until now there hasn't been anyone I've wanted to. The boys who go to my high school look like they've jumped into a pile of dirty laundry and swum up wearing clothes two or three sizes too big. They carry an aroma of old sweat and mold. I am a sophomore, so I have two and a half more years of this to look forward to. Still, a lot of girls have gone way far past kissing, and Kathy and I sometimes feel like we need remediation.

"Do you still want to talk to the judge about not living with your father?" Kathy asks, after we're done laughing at the kissing article.

"I don't know," I say. "Sometimes. But then I come here, and I don't want to be here either."

"It's too bad we can't just run away," Kathy says.

"Why should you want to run away? You've got nice parents. They let you do things. They drop you off at school and pick you up. Your dad even goes to movies with you. I wish my dad would do that."

"Sometimes, I just think I want to get away," Kathy says. "So I could just live the way I want to. Nobody telling me to clean up my room. I could just let everything pile up a foot deep."

"It's already a foot deep."

"OK, then," she says, "two feet."

Really, Kathy's room is utter chaos. Leonard and Dad would both kill me if my room got like that.

I lied to Dr. Grewal about boys. There is one, sort of. Gustave—not his real name—spikes his hair with egg whites and bleaches the spikes only far enough down so that you can definitely see the roots are black. You'd expect him to smell like a rotten egg by 3:00, but he doesn't. His real name is Jason Dulgy, but in French class we have French names—I'm Camille—and that's where he asked me, French class. He just said, "Mon chérie, can I be your boyfriend?"

He's one of the biggest clowns in class, so I assume he's just fitting me into his comedy routine. "My father won't let me go out with anyone who puts albumin in his hair."

He looked surprised. "I never use albumin, Camille. Just egg whites."

"I'm sorry," I said.

He looked so disappointed.

"You're serious," I said.

"Mais oui, mam'selle."

"It's not you, or anything. My dad just doesn't want me hanging out with guys. He says he doesn't want me going on 'dates' yet."

"Yeah?" I think Gustave thought I was lying to him.

"It's true," I said.

"We don't have to do anything special. I mean, nobody goes on 'dates.'"

He's skinny, but he has nice eyes and he's smart, even though he's ignorant. We're both in honors chemistry, too.

"OK," I said.

We're lab partners now. I wonder what it would be like to kiss Jason Dulgy. I can't say I dream about it.

How can I describe my father? It's like he's always standing in back of me.

In eighth grade I went to junior high camp at Lake Onagaming, just for three days. Daddy came along as a counselor. Kathy's dad volunteered too. One day the climbing instructors—they stay with the camp all summer—took us to a cliff. Not a big cliff, and for most of the way down, really, just a slanted piece of rock.

All afternoon, we rappelled down that cliff. I went three times. The two climbing instructors were at the top, and Dad was at the bottom. Nobody asked him to be at the bottom, he just was. He took over. He made sure everyone had their gear on right. Their helmets on. He wouldn't let anyone stand around the place where people landed when they were rappelling, children, or even adults: "Move back. Move back a little. There."

Dad talks all the time, and he wears people out. I could tell he was wearing Kathy's dad out. People don't like to be bossed around and told what to do, but Dad was in his element, voicing his opinions to Kathy's dad about kids and girls in junior high who wear skimpy two-piece bathing suits and act like sluts.

That morning, we had been on a climbing wall, on one of the cabins. Kathy's dad went to the top, but my dad didn't even try. That's when he started taking over in his panicky way. He doesn't like heights, so he didn't rappel either, but he worked it out by deputizing himself climbing instuctor number three: Sir Edmund Hillary.

"Why does Dad always want to control everything?" I asked my mother once. She said that when she first knew him, she liked it, because it made her feel protected, but that later, she just felt trapped. I don't know if she realized she hadn't answered my question.

Last year. Dad is sweaty from playing basketball and inflated with anger. His face an overripe tomato, ready to split.

"You're too young to go to a dance."

"I'm fifteen."

"Too young."

"Practically everyone I know is going with someone."

"You're not everybody. You're my daughter, and I don't want you acting like the rest of those girls."

"What do you mean, like the rest?"

"I've seen them. They're like little sluts, putting on make-up. . . ."

"So I have to wait how long? A year?"

"No."

"I can't go to a dance when I'm a junior in high school?"

"No."

"When, then? When I'm eighteen?"

"When I say you can."

"When I go to college? Is that when?"

"Don't get smart with me."

"When I go to college, just how are you going to stop me?"

"I'll go to college with you if I have to."

"You want to keep me all to yourself."

"Yes." His blue eyes bulge.

"Well, doesn't that make you some kind of pervert?"

That's when he hits me. Really gets his weight into it. One instant I'm by the kitchen counter, close to the blender, and the next, I'm across the room, my head smack against the handle of a drawer, the world pulsing in and out. I start to cry, and the twins come in and start to cry, but Martha shoos them out of the kitchen, and I hear a door close at the back of the house.

My father looks down at me, stricken.

He stoops, and I jerk away, but I can't get off the floor. He folds me in his arms and his stinky, sweaty T-shirt. I hate being enclosed like this, having my arms pinned to my sides. It makes me panicky, and I start to breathe hard. "Daddy . . . Daddy . . . please."

"I'm sorry. I'm so sorry. Why did you make me do that? Don't make me do that anymore. Why did you do that? Don't make me do that anymore," he says, over and over, as he rocks me, my arms pinned to my sides.

"Daddy. I won't . . . please. Please let me get up," I croak. "I'm choking. I think I'm going to be sick." He gets up quickly. His sweat is all over me, like dog slobber. I go around him, out the screen door. I don't go to school for three days, until the black and blue are nearly gone.

If knocking me across the kitchen was the worst thing my father ever did, I suppose it's only fair to put down the best thing too, which was to give me a telescope for my birthday and help me focus in on the moon, and Jupiter and Saturn. I love him the most when I think of standing next to him on warm summer nights, taking turns looking through the telescope. He's an airplane mechanic for United, and for the last couple years, he's been working on a mechanical engineering degree. He loves anything that requires precision. One night he explained the Doppler effect to me, which I've read about since in astronomy books.

The Doppler effect has to do with the frequency at which an observer receives waves—say sound or light waves. If the source of the waves is approaching you, the waves come closer and closer together. For instance, picture yourself on Route 18. Elvis is driving toward you in his Cadillac convertible with his band in the backseat, and they're getting down about how Elvis has a hunk of burning love he wants to give some lucky girl. As he approaches, his song gets more high-pitched, and the hunks come faster and faster, as if you were hearing a record slowly speeded up from 33 ⅓ rpms to 78. As he whizzes past you, the song hits its climax, so to speak, and gradually goes back from 78 to 33 ⅓. This has never actually happened to me on Route 18. On Route 18, Elvis is always sitting beside me, in my little convertible sports car, and when he sings he sounds normally passionate, for Elvis anyway, because he is a stationary source for the sound. Off Route 18, though, life seems to go by me like a Doppler effect, one where the frequency speeds up like crazy for a few weeks and then slows down for months and finally moves to the beat of a paralytic drummer.

It wasn't the smack in the face that was the worst part of when Dad attacked me. It was having my arms pinned. I get scared to death about that. Even when I was little and my mother used to tuck me in, if she'd lean on the bed, with both her hands planted by my elbows, so I couldn't move my arms, I'd get panicked and want to scream.

I have a memory. It must be from when I was two or three. I

think that I've come home from the grocery store with my mother, and that I've been a perfect little beast. I think I wanted something at the checkout counter, and when she said no, I screamed. Or maybe I just threw a temper tantrum at home.

The next thing I remember is this big old red couch we used to have, which is scratchy because the fabric is sculpted and some is rough and stands up from the rest. I'm on the couch, and I'm screaming, and Mommy takes a pillow and puts it over my mouth and pushes down on it with all her might. She pushes me down into the couch cushion.

I can't move. I can't even struggle, or breathe. It's very dark. The pillow is molded to me, around my face, my arms, even my mouth. No matter how hard I strain, I cannot move. The only thing that's moving is my mind, and its getting ready to explode from the pressure of trying to move my arms. Then the pillow comes away, and there's Mommy, like a white sheet with eyes painted on it. I lie there, a gaping fish, unable, for an instant, to move my arms or breathe.

Not long ago I told my mother I remembered this. "It's just your imagination," she said sharply. "It never happened. Children can't remember back that far."

"Then why am I always so scared when my arms get pinned?"

"Linda," she says, "what a hateful thing to say." She's mad, not sorry, so at first I think maybe she really didn't do it. If she had, wouldn't I see something in her eyes, some kind of guilt or regret?

I love the song "Route 66" and wish Route 18 had its own song. I'd like to make one up, but I can't seem to do it. I came across "Route 66" when I was six or seven, and Mom and Dad were screaming at each other in the bedroom. That's when they were trying to hide their hatred from me. The yelling made all the walls in the house vibrate. Later that summer, they were screaming in the kitchen, the living room, everywhere, and I was hearing words like *slut* and *whore* for the first time.

Anyway, I was looking at a blank TV screen. Usually I couldn't move when they got that way. I was afraid of what would happen if they noticed me, and I would strain to hear what they were saying, because I thought it might be about me, that maybe I'd caused their anger. But that day—I don't know why—I turned on the TV very low. I was flicking around on the channel changer, and I hit one of those cable stations that just show old TV shows like *Leave It to Beaver* and *The Andy Griffith Show*. I saw these two guys jumping into a convertible sports car, a little thing that looked like an elongated Volkswagen bug. "Route 66" was playing in the background. I liked those two guys, Martin Milner and George Maharis, and I just rode away with them. They had adventures wherever they stopped, but they could always keep moving, and as long as they did, they were OK. Driving was the purest, most pleasant thing they did. I don't know why they ever stopped, except for gas and sleep, and because it was a TV program, and something's got to happen. I could have just watched them drive, endlessly, and I imagined myself on the road with them, sometimes in the backseat, sometimes up front. Whatever kind of car they had, it's the one I drive on Route 18. In black and white, their car was light-colored, and maybe that's why my own is almost always yellow, a flying banana that has a black ball on the end of the stick shift.

Around this time I got into making maps. I'd draw imaginary countries and cattle ranches on typing paper, and I decided, why not make my own highway? I'd show my maps to Mom and Dad, if they were having a good day, and they'd smile at me and tell me how good my maps were. I'd draw maps until there was no more paper in the house, and nobody complained. For Christmas, Daddy got me a Rand McNally road atlas of the United States. He really liked the idea of a daughter who drew maps. He said it showed that I would grow up to be a scientist or an engineer. The road atlas had a map of the United States as a whole and one for each state. I drew Route 18 right into the road atlas. It took me weeks. My road meanders through every state in the union and goes through some of them twice. It starts in Hoboken, goes through New York City on the way to Montauk Point, and then travels in a loop and a crescent to Cape Cod. From there it goes up to New England, and back south, all the way to the Florida Keys, where the islands are connected by some of the world's longest suspension bridges. Then it jogs back up through Georgia and winds its way like a drugged snake, north to south, back and forth, over the rest of the country. I tried to figure out how long it was once, and I came up with about thirty-five thousand miles (I used a string to trace it and then measured the inches on the string).

The speed limit on Route 18 varies. On some stretches, you can go as fast as you want. I started out driving it with Martin Milner and George Maharis, but I've had various companions, and my favorite is Elvis Presley, when we sing along with his songs on the radio. I like driving with Eddie Rabbitt too.

Stepparents are supposed to be more dangerous than real ones. I've read books about it. Because your genetic parents have more of a genetic investment in you, the theory goes, they are much more likely to take care of you. But for stepparents, you're just a competitor for resources they'd like to give their own kids. Stepparents are the ones you've got to watch out for, just like in that movie *The Stepfather* or in fairy tales, like "Hansel and Gretel" or "Cinderella." In my life this theory has turned out to be bullshit. The adults who are really dangerous are the ones who see you as a walking genetic legacy.

Martha's nicer to me than my real mom, and Leonard's an asshole, but he's not dangerous. One day I came home from school, and Leonard was in the driveway putting a new license plate on the back of the car. He crouched, twisting his screwdriver. His 36" jeans had slid way down his ass, which they do when he squats, and he was flashing the neighborhood a hairy white half-moon. You'd think there'd be a point of no return right about there, an event horizon where his pants would slide off altogether. How does a man's ass stay so skinny when his belly hangs over his belt like a squishy weather balloon? I'd rather live dangerously than have any of Leonard's genes.

Then there's my father, who loves me but knocked me across

the kitchen, and my mother, who loves me, too, but tried to off me with a pillow. Of course, children aren't easy. I can see how, as a mother, your kid might drive you so crazy that, for an instant, you might lose control and want to kill her. I have four kids, two at each house, to baby-sit, and they get on my nerves. I love them, but then they're not mine. And now I'm sharing my rooms with three little girls. I don't feel like strangling them, but sometimes, if I could just have a room to myself, it would be even better than driving alone on Route 18. I don't ever want to have kids. I don't ever want to feel like killing them.

In November of my sophomore year, Dad decides the whole psychiatrist adventure has been bad for me. I stop seeing Dr. Grewal, and Dad takes my Paxil away. He says the stuff is poison— all kinds of bad side effects. Besides, I don't have to be depressed if I don't want to be. Being happy is just a decision, and I have to quit moping around and make it. It starts one morning after breakfast when I go to the medicine cabinet, and Dad's in the bathroom, barring the door, the little orange cylinder wrapped in his fist.

"Dad, I need that stuff."

"I don't want you to get addicted."

"Dad, it's medicine! I'll crash without it."

I can't pry it out of his hands. He has all the virtue of a parent who has discovered cocaine in his daughter's dresser. Tough love, I can hear him thinking. *Gotta give that girl tough love.* Like most people, he assigns himself dramatic parts and gets caught up in them.

That week I come down like an airplane whose wings have fallen off. You can't go off Paxil cold. The world Dopplers to a crawl, a definite red shift, as the stars and planets recede in the distance. I can't think. I can't remember. I'm first-chair clarinet in band, and I can barely move my fingers over the keys. My head aches so bad the roots of my hair hurt. The band director's baton moves like a baseball bat, and I think my head is going to roll off my shoulders. I can't tell when the shock from going off the drug starts and the depression begins. I just want to sit in my bedroom and stare at the wall, and that is what I would do if people let me alone, but they pursue me, relentlessly. Do the dishes. Change the baby's diaper. I drag myself around the house at my mother's and father's, wondering how much more it could hurt to just plunge a bread knife into my heart and stop the whole thing.

I pop Advil for the headaches and get as much caffeine as I can. At home I drink coffee, and at school, Gustave helps me out, bringing me an extra couple bucks each day to buy Coke and Mountain Dew and Dr. Pepper, and it helps a little, I think, and Gustave is so sweet, keeps me from crashing through the earth into some lower level of darkness; Dante knew what he was talking about—the ninth level of hell being made of ice where everything stops, frozen. What will I do when the other phase starts, and I'm jitterbugging around the house, up all hours, putting my room one way and then the other, talking like a machine gun—what then?

I hold myself together through an internal system of ropes and pulleys that keep me from flying apart or crashing into myself like an imploding beer can. I eventually nag my mother into letting me stay over at Kathy's house. It's impossible for her to withstand me when I get like this because I don't let up, can't, and next week I'm likely to be comatose, so I'm making the most out of my energy while I have it. I've even told her that I'm going to a dance, the winter formal, and since my mother can take anything but pressure, she collapses on that too, and even gets into it, gets me a dress, like she remembers I'm sixteen and she's my mother, and maybe we're both missing something, though she knows my father's going to be hopping mad if he ever finds out, and she'll take all kinds of shit, and Leonard hates it when I'm distracting her, and she's spending money on me. But like I said, when she knows I'm going, she gets into it, even helps me pick out a dress, and pays for it, black and sort of slinky, perfect for a winter formal, which is a little formal, a prom warm-up. I've even told her that Gustave and Kevin are coming to pick us up at Kathy's house at 7:45.

⟶⊹⟵

Kathy and I have been getting ready for a while, baths, make-up, hiding out in Kathy's bedroom, ready to make a grand appearance. I help Kathy put her hair up. She always likes to wear it "up" in some kind of elaborate concoction of twists and turns that she gets from this book, something like *One Hundred and One Ways to Twist Your Hair Around*. She has fine blond hair, and strands of it always get loose, so she has that partially disheveled look that boys drool over. Now, one strand bobs around her eyelash, and her blue eyes make her look impish. She's really beautiful. I have a big Armenian nose, like my mom, and my hair is long. I just brush it out. Kathy says I look like an Indian princess. I don't know about the princess part, but I feel good when I look at the two of us in the mirror.

"Better than mortal man deserves," she says as we gaze at ourselves. She likes to steal lines from movies. That one's from *The Terminator*.

"Look at the lovely ladies," Kathy's dad says when we emerge from the bedroom side of the house. He makes a big deal out of us. So does Kathy's mom. It's corny, but it makes me feel good, and I can feel tears coming to my eyes, that people can be so generous as to spend affection as if it weren't in short supply.

I wonder if Gustave will want to kiss me. I don't even want to think about what it would be like to run my fingers through Gustave's hair. I'm afraid some of his spikes might break off. But when Kevin and Gustave come to the door, they have been transformed too. Gustave's stalagmite hair is gone, though it's still bleached out and the black roots show. "I got tired of egg whites," he mumbles.

"No. His mother made him do it," Kevin grins while Gustave scowls to hide his embarrassment.

The dance is in the school gym. Colored lights. Punch. Parents chaperoning. Kids hanging out in the parking lot, talking, or standing at the sidelines of the gym. I dance with Gustave, Kevin; some of the other guys ask me. It's not like I'm that attached to anyone. I'm free, and it's nice. Some of the girls are in incredible dresses. A lot of rich kids go to our high school. They drive their

BMWs to school and keep their golf clubs in the trunks, and most of them have that superior attitude that so often goes with money. But tonight, they can't irritate me, and I enjoy watching them in their beautiful gowns and tuxedos. It's almost as if they have their own formal going on, one of the cogs spinning around the dance floor, in a particular part of the gym. The black kids have theirs, the Hispanic kids theirs, though the groups do mix some. Kathy and I are part of the lower-to-middling group, the girls jiggling around the dance floor in something close to fifty or sixty dollars, or homemade, our own regenerating wheel of couples.

Gustave isn't a bad dancer. He's wiry and a little tight when he moves. I like to think I'm lithe. I may be kidding myself, but I don't care. When I dance with Gustave, I don't have to worry about how I look. He's a comfortable person to be around. Will he kiss me tonight, or will he seize up? In junior high, we timed Amy Herwood and John Novatny to see how long they could kiss each other, and they went for over ninety seconds until one of the playground teachers came over and saw what was going on. They got expelled. It was just a stunt, of course, but I've often wondered how it must have felt to press your lips to someone else's for that long. I don't know when Gustave is going to get the chance to kiss me. When he and Kevin drop off Kathy and me, I don't suppose we can all just stand outside her door kissing each other.

About halfway through the dance, I decide it is time to give Gustave some encouragement. "It's awfully hot in here," I say after one of the dances. "Maybe we should get some fresh air."

"OK," he says.

Outside it's cold and a little foggy. We walk out in the parking lot, and I'm surprised there are so many people, some just talking, some kissing, as if no one else on earth existed. They know they're under observation though. High school is a big drama, and out here some are playing to the crowd, saying, *Look what I've got, or look what I can do: I'm a man. I'm a woman. Yippee.*

"Let's walk out on the grass," I say.

Gustave and I walk toward the tennis courts, over the field

where the girl's soccer team practices and plays its games. The ground is hard and the grass brittle with cold. A maple tree casts a long black shadow against the floodlit ground. Beneath the tree, it is both light and dark at the same time, and I want Gustave to press me up against the bark and kiss me for ninety seconds. He doesn't though. He just stands around flat-footed, and I'm almost ready for him to start scuffing his shoes in the dirt and saying "Gosh." He's getting the signal all right—he just doesn't know whether he ought to believe it. He's not dense. He just doesn't want to make a mistake, and I take that for politeness. So I put my arms around his neck and kiss him. At first his spine is rigid as a broom handle, but then he's kissing me, and my heart is banging against my rib cage, and I feel the earthworms waking up beneath my feet, fooled into thinking it's spring.

Gustave and Kevin drop us off at Kathy's, and we stand around on the porch for awhile, and Kevin gives Kathy a chaste peck on the cheek, and Gustave, taking the cue, does the same to me. I feel lighter than I have in months, even without the Paxil. I'm not stupid enough to think I'm in love with Gustave, or he with me, but I feel relaxed and happy with him, and I can't think of another male that would apply to. Kathy's dad makes her feel that way. It's because she knows what to expect of him. It's after 12:00, and he is up and waiting for us. He's sitting at the kitchen table reading a magazine when we come in the door. He smiles at us, though he looks a little uneasy, and says, "How was the dance?"

Kathy gives him the standard answer: "Oh. It was OK."

Then he looks at me. "Your father called, Linda. About half an hour ago. He's coming to pick you up."

"But I'm spending the weekend with my mother," I say, more to myself than anyone else. I can feel tears coming, and I don't want to cry. Why would my mother have told him? I can almost hear the conversation over the phone. "Where's Linda?" he keeps demanding. She just collapses whenever he starts grilling her, and Leonard never wants me around anyway. He wouldn't encourage her to stand up to Dad. It's always just easiest for her to give in.

Was he mad? I want to ask, but it's too humiliating. Besides, I can feel his rage moving up the highway. His daughter has given him the slip, gone to a dance, planned to spend the night with a friend, and it'll be the last time, he'll tell me. The last time you ever pull a stunt like that.

Kathy takes me back to her bedroom, and I do start to cry. She just keeps passing me the Kleenex. I can't even change out of my dress. It would be better if I could—get into some jeans and a sweatshirt, the kind of clothes that are not likely to rouse my father's ire, but when he sees this silky dress, with the slit in the side, modest as it is, he'll talk about teenage sluts for days. How he's not going to let his daughter become one, despite her obvious desire to display herself. And maybe, tomorrow, when he starts to think about it more, works himself up more and more, he'll belt me. Just smack me across the living room or the kitchen again, and it'll be finals week, and then what will I do? What lie this time? I picture myself on the floor, in a kitchen corner, my face throbbing, my father, all repentant, bending down to pick me up. And that's when I ram the bread knife into his guts, the long serrated one, and I just keep twisting and sawing, and won't let go. . . .

Kathy gets me out of the dress into a sweatshirt and jeans.

"Why don't you call your mom?" Kathy says. "He's got no right to get you. This isn't his week. Maybe your Mom doesn't even know he's coming to get you."

I realize I'm so disappointed Mom has told him about the dance that I don't care what happens to me.

Kathy says, "You can't buy into your dad's shit about you. Don't let that negative shit get inside you." But I have. I'm like a stuffed turkey, filled to the throat with my father and mother's negative shit.

When Dad comes to the front door there is no scene. Kathy's dad opens the door, smiles, says, "Hi." My dad smiles back, and I scoot out like a black cat slipping under a garage door just before it shuts. Not a word passes between Dad and me for about ten minutes. I just hear the sounds of traffic, the car's engine, the heater blowing. Then he starts slowly. About how not telling him about the dance was like lying to him. About how my mother used to lie to him, and now I'm doing it, just like she did. He doesn't ask me what I wore. But he will. He's slow, like a machine that takes rock and grinds it into fine powder. He's got time, all weekend, and he'll use it. He's studying to be an engineer after all, and engineers are thorough, methodical types.

We pass farmhouses on the outskirts of Trenton, fields, bare and exhausted. My father hasn't shaved today. He often skips on the weekends. The lower half of his face almost disappears in the dark car, but his eyes and temples go white in the gleam of lights. I can't look at him. I can't even look at the road.

I close my eyes, and after a while, the texture of the road changes. I can hear and feel the wheels bite into a rougher grade of asphalt. I look, and a wheat field nods in the slow evening breeze. We pass a cornfield, and the big flat leaves slap against each other like knives. There is rain in the air. No oncoming traffic. In the distance heat lightning flashes, and among it, like subaudible thunder, my father rumbles away. Signs flash by. Route 18. Speed Limit 75. The steering wheel vibrates beneath my hands. The clean, heavy summer air brushes my hair back and blows through my pores. I head into the lightning and reach for the radio. I love a rainy night.

PERFECTION IN BAD AXE

For Frank O'Dell, Wednesday night in Bad Axe is the chiming chaos of bowling pins, scattering and crashing at Huron Lanes. Each impact has its own musical configuration. And like the church bells around town, clanging indifferently to each other on a Good Friday afternoon, these separate strikings create an unplanned harmony. Laughter, voices, automatic pinsetters, balls returning, balls rolling down the bright, waxed wood—all combine to drop a gauzy curtain of sound over the sharper music of collision.

Frank O'Dell is my father, and tonight he is hot, so things are looking up for the McVey's Insurance team. His first game was a 230, and his second, a 243. He is into the fifth frame of his third game and has bowled five strikes in a row. He has never bowled a perfect game, and he wonders what it would feel like. He tells himself to stop thinking about it. His teammates want to get him a ginger ale, and he almost shakes his head no, afraid any distracting sensation, even drinking pop, will take him out of the groove; but he realizes if he starts to take the game that seriously, he'll probably screw up anyway. So he says yes to the ginger ale so as *not* to screw up his concentration. They bring him a Vernor's, and as he waits his turn, he takes a good long swallow. He flexes the practiced fingers of his right hand and extends them as if he were already holding the ball.

•—◄❖►—•

Before Dad even started his first game, the Seventh Day Adventist minister's son, Larry Horgan, was pouring coins out of the jelly jar where his mother kept her spare change. Larry's paychecks from the A&P went in the bank, so he had no spending money, thus keeping opportunities to sin to a minimum. He took two dimes, five pennies, and a quarter from his mother's change jar.

He'd decided to go to the Bad Axe Theater. It had red and blue neon lights, which outlined the words *Bad Axe* and the shape of a broken hatchet. He had never been inside the theater, which people in Bad Axe simply called "the show," though it had exerted an awful pull on him. Larry's church didn't allow watching movies or television, dancing, drinking, or card-playing. Bowling and billiards were too far beyond the pale to need mention. But *West Side Story* had been rereleased, and he wanted to see it. For a week, he had gazed at the posters featuring Natalie Wood, and she was the most beautiful creature he had ever seen. Tonight was the last showing. His parents were driving to Tri-City airport to pick up a visiting missionary from Africa. They'd left early to make time for an uncharacteristic indulgence: dinner in the Sky Room. It was almost as if God were giving Larry a chance to see the movie, which, Larry admitted to himself, seemed unlikely. But whether this happy concurrence of events was of divine or satanic origin, Larry intended to make the most of it. With the show starting at 7:00, he'd have plenty of time to get home before his parents returned from the airport, seventy miles away. His mother wouldn't miss the change. He went out the door into the clean, clear air. Just a few snowflakes were coming down, and he joyfully kicked his way through the little drift in the front yard.

Al McLean looks like a human bowling ball, the Vernor's gnome, a tobacco-stained Santa Claus, moonlighting during the off-season as a bowling proprietor. He has a round, tight belly and curly black sideburns, much longer than the style. He wears the same colorless pants and shirts every day, and green-gray suspenders, always suspenders. Children are in awe of him. He is five feet, six inches tall. He is the dwarf, the underground creature who makes the bowling alley work, though no one knows how. He is the owner of Huron Lanes, never without a cigar between his thumb and forefinger. He holds his cigar that way because that's how his father held his. Holding a cigar between your fingers is effeminate, something a cigarette smoker might do.

Many people who have bowled at Huron Lanes for years have never actually seen Al put a cigar to his mouth. However, the butts of his cigars pile up in ashtrays at the front desk, next to the brass cash register, so people guess he must be smoking them. Dad has known Al for years, gone deer hunting with him every fall, and actually seen Al take drags off his cigars, but Al seems more interested in adding smoke to the general atmosphere than in taking it directly into his lungs. A lot of the time, Al's cigar goes out, but he still holds it, for an hour at a time, telling customers slow stories in his rumbly basso profundo voice. They have heard all the stories before. Al knows he's probably told the same people the same stories, though he is never quite sure. He is willing to take the risk, however. His stories add necessary ritual to the bowling alley, a proper rhythm, the liturgy of a Wednesday night. Al is the least hurried man in town, and when people are around him, they can't hurry either, and mostly don't want to.

While my father was on the fifth frame of his still-perfect game, I was not quite dead drunk in the snowladen shrubs directly in front of Al McLean's house. I had been seized with grief over what I'd done to his wife, Clara, a few months before, and was staggering toward his home to apologize once again—to apologize more effectively. But as I trudged across his front yard, the world tilted on its side, and I found myself on the ground, faceup, staring into the infinite lines of falling snow, each flake leaving a vapor trail behind as it fell to earth. The shrubs had dumped several handfuls of snow down the front of my shirt, and my body was going into deep freeze. I could hear the minute chiming of big snowflakes bumping into each other. It was like the sound you hear at wedding receptions, when the guests are all tapping spoons against wineglasses, urging the bride and groom to kiss, but it was much fainter, more melodic, and contained no urgency whatsoever. I'd never heard the chiming of snowflakes before, and I felt quite content to listen and slowly fall asleep. But before I fall asleep and wake up in Hubbard Memorial Hospital, I must go back to an earlier point in the day, before the league bowling at Huron Lanes, before Larry rips off his mom to go to the movies—even before I've had my first drink.

I was working at the A&P with Larry Horgan, just getting off, and as usual we stopped at Jim's Pure Service across the street. I got some potato chips to split with Larry. Inside, we sat on low ledges by the plate-glass windows, talked, and watched cars pull up belching white clouds into the winter air. The kids who pumped gas for Jim were friends of mine, mostly high school football players, who, unlike me, hadn't been caught drinking. Customers left their cars and came in to talk. The cold little room reeked of gas and oil, and we blew on our lightly fisted hands to warm them up.

You could find out anything at Jim's, and Larry and I liked to be in the know. Information (not gossip) was passed back and forth constantly. Did you hear about the four couples engaged in "wife-swapping" in town? The mechanics and gas pumpers at Jim's could fill you in. Were you interested in the last time the Baptist minister beat his wife? Who your cute French teacher slept with a couple nights ago? Jim's had the answers. The place held another attraction for me: if you were under twenty-one and wanting some liquor for Friday night, Jim's son, Jimmy the Bomb, just out of the Marine Corps, had no problem picking up a bottle or two for you at the liquor store on the east side of town.

It was this little feature of Jim's that made the place especially valuable to me. At sixteen, I liked to drink on the weekends. The previous spring, I'd gotten kicked off the football team for illegal possession. Dumb luck. I'd been in a car with a bunch of other guys; they'd had some beer, and we got stopped. I'd had one can of Stroh's. Kids caught drinking were not allowed to play sports for a year. So I got a job at the A&P, and spent my time other ways.

Jimmy the Bomb had agreed to get me a couple bottles of Black and White Scotch for the weekend, but I'd asked him to pick it up on Wednesday, because I was working 'til 9:00 on Friday night. My drinking was creeping into the week.

He said, "What's wrong with Friday after 9:00?"

I said, "I don't want to mess up your Friday night."

He said, "I'm not doing anything."

I said, "Well, I'll have to go home after work and change—just thought this might be easier."

He shrugged, looked at me a little funny. But ex-Marines didn't bug future Marines about their drinking habits, and when Larry and I got to Jim's Pure after work, he had the booze, which I transferred, carefully, from his old Dodge pickup to an A&P supermarket bag. Larry, who was with me, frowned but said nothing.

"When are you going to have a drink, Deacon?" Jimmy laughed and squeezed Larry's shoulder.

"You're Catholic," Larry said. "You've got a long tradition of wine-bibbing in your church. We use grape juice."

Larry was OK by Jim, though Larry had a long face, a serious demeanor, and was unfortunately twisted up in his family's religion—hence "Deacon," a nickname Larry had acquired in junior high.

"I have high hopes for you yet," Jim said. "You sure you don't want something?"

Larry shook his head.

"Well," Jimmy nodded at me, "Doug here's got plenty for the both of you."

Larry went home. I went to Charlie Gorr's house to drink. Charlie's dad ran the local pool hall in the basement under Clevenger's; it had an ugly assortment of warped tables and cue sticks, but the disreputable men who played there factored in all the curves. Mr. Gorr was seldom home, and neither he nor Flora, Charlie's mother, much cared what their son did, though Flora complained about how much Charlie ate. Flora was wiry and strong, as thin as her son was fat, and she had the vilest mouth

I've ever known on a woman. Charlie was my age and must have weighed three hundred pounds. A few weeks before, I'd watched Charlie eat a whole pecan pie by himself. His mother had made it for Christmas, and Charlie just sat down and ate it by the giant spoonful. He didn't offer me any.

"Jee-zus!" Flora said when she came in the kitchen and saw Charlie scarfing down the pie, "You're getting so fat you got tits like a woman." Then she grabbed one of them and squeezed. Charlie, his gullet full of pecan pie, could only utter a strangulated yelp and try to get away. But she dug her talons into Charlie's boob like a giant staple remover. He got up and yowled, jigged around the kitchen, shaking this way and that, bellowing, while Flora was whipped around like a noodle. Finally, she let go. "Don't go eating my fuckin' pies unless I say you can, lard ass," she said. Charlie sat down, massaged his breast, and finished the pie.

Any form of gluttony and retaliation was possible in the Gorr household. Flora was English and had found her husband during the war. She didn't see anything wrong with taking a couple shots of gin to start the day. She was a steady drinker, but I never saw her drunk. You can have a drink every hour or so and float through the day in a pleasantly sodden haze. I enjoyed feeling that way and had drifted rather easily into the Gorr household. So my next stop, after Jim's Pure, was Charlie's. I put the scotch on the kitchen table, Charlie got a couple glasses and a euchre deck, and Flora came out of the living room, where she had been watching *The Price Is Right,* her nose twitching with excitement. "Black and White," she said, "my favorite." She went to the cupboard and got out a giant jar of Planter's salted nuts and slammed them on the table, as if to say, let's get going. Sometimes Flora ran out of money for booze, and this must have been one of her dry spells, because she started drinking with unusual gusto, and I felt I had to keep up to protect my investment. Charlie, of course, matched us, and before long the peanuts and most of the first bottle were gone. What the hell, I thought. I owed Flora a few drinks. We dipped into bottle number two. We were playing Shoot the

Moon, and cards flew across the table. Charlie and I kept forgetting what was trump. By the time Larry walked into *West Side Story*, I was reeling.

The first thing Larry noticed was the smell of popcorn. Mr.
Pell, a frail, bent little man with a bald head, who'd run the theater for years, took his ticket. Larry stepped into a hallway, which
had a long "window" covered with burgundy velvet curtains. On
crowded nights, if you came early to the nine o'clock show, and
the seven o'clock hadn't let out yet, you could get in and watch
the ending of the movie by pushing those curtains aside, or by going to either end of the hall, where the aisles come out. Few people did this—if they came in early, they listened to the soundtrack
but avoided peeking at the show. I heard the whole battle of Fort
Knox at the end of *Goldfinger* without peeking, but it was a damn
strain. Larry was one of those who'd never peek.

He entered the theater. The house lights were still up. All the
seats were empty. Larry took a spot in the very center and waited for people to come in. He enjoyed the silence. The light hair on
his forearms rose in the charged air. Larry scrunched down, a little afraid someone would recognize him, but then realized no one
from his church would come, or if they did, they couldn't accuse
him of debauchery without implicating themselves. He relaxed a
little, and no one came; no, on a Wednesday night, was interested in seeing a rereleased *West Side Story*. This show, Larry
realized, was just for him. The lights went off, the blue clock over
the left exit glowed, and the first atonal, whistling strains of *West
Side Story* made Larry shiver as the New York skyline began to
take shape.

Flora knew every card that was out, and I finished owing her
five and a half bucks. While Maria and Tony were singing
"Tonight," I was trying to get down the unshoveled and icy steps
of the Gorr's back porch without falling. My stomach churned,
the world wobbled, and I wanted to upchuck into the bushes that
struggled for life in the Gorr's backyard. The fastest way home

was down main street, Huron Avenue, but I was not going to go that way, because I was falling-down drunk. I heard the door open behind me. "You forgot your hat, Dougie," Flora said, and threw it to me in a loopy overhand. It sailed over my head. "Shit," she said, and backed unsteadily into the house. I heard the door slam.

I made it to the hat, bent over to get it, and my stomach gave up the scotch that hadn't already entered my bloodstream. I left the mess and started to stagger home "the back way," down the residential streets of Bad Axe, past the elementary school and Sacred Heart Church. I longed for mouthwash. Dad was in the middle of his second game, Al McLean was presiding over a seamless night of league bowling, Larry had entered that state where man and movie are one, and Maria had convinced Tony he had to stop the fight between Bernardo and Riff. Al McLean's wife, Clara, reclined on the sofa, watching TV. The arthritis in her knee and the tightness in her ribs made moving harder for her. She didn't go to the bowling alley as often as she used to, when she was a jolly companion to her husband. No. She pretty much hung out at home, tired, different than she had been before, and it was my fault.

I changed direction and headed toward Clara.

By the time Dad gets to the eighth frame of his third game, he is still perfect. A buzz has gone round the bowling alley, and more and more bowlers, as they finish their turns, drift over to watch, and then go back to their own games. Al has the best spot, and he isn't budging. He and Dad used to bowl in tournaments in Chicago, and he's almost as excited about this game as Dad, who is talking to himself in his head, trying not to think himself out of his streak. He's thinking, *Don't think. Don't think.*

A bowler on the Farm Bureau team picks up a split, and then it's Dad's turn. He gets his ball, rolls his shoulders around and then his head. He sets, willing his mind to go blank. There is only a motion to make, and that he must not think about. He must not even think about starting to move. He must not think about not thinking. He pauses on the alley, like a statue, *Man the Bowler,* until all else dies away, and then his left foot moves forward; he takes fives steps, a little shuffle, and the ball is on the alley, Dad's arm curving to the ceiling in a graceful follow-through. He stops, fixed in space, and then becomes a spectator, like everyone else. The ball seems too far to the right, rolling, rolling to a split, but it arcs back, into the pocket. Pins fly all over the place, trying to find other pins to knock down, but it's like Dad's thrown a hand grenade—the pins just disappear in the blast. McVey's Insurance cheers. The Farm Bureau team cheers. "'At a way, boy!" Al McLean shouts.

I made progress slowly toward Clara McLean, a fifteen-minute walk that stretched into half an hour and longer. My dizzy spells got worse and worse. I leaned against the elm trees, their cold tacky bark hard against my cheek. I progressed by sprint, from tree to tree, and at each tree I hung on for awhile, until I got where I needed to go. The air barely stirred, but the night was cold, and my windbreaker did little to keep me warm. I had no gloves and didn't want to think about my hat.

The McLeans lived in a typical house for Bad Axe. It was probably fifty years old, at least, had two stories and a front porch. As I walked across the yard I imagined that Jack Frost had drawn his skittering diagrams across the inside of my veins. I had never felt so painfully cold. My eyes spun, the world upended, and I found myself sprawled in the shrubs.

Light from the house escaped the curtains and fell across my legs. I thought, *Why not rest for awhile? I must straighten my thoughts before I talk to Clara.* I nestled my head into the snow and watched the tipsy flakes fall to earth. I listened to their music. The world no longer threatened to flip over and dump me into space. *I'm sorry,* I thought. *There must be something I can say besides "I'm sorry."*

I recalled the day, six months before, when I'd run into Clara McLean. I was in a bike race, a race that had sprung out of nothing. No challenges had been issued, no finish line specified. The evening air was like silk, and I was with Larry Horgan and a couple other guys, all of us just a few months short of getting our driver's licenses. We were peddling south on North Port Crescent, poking along, and one of the guys, with a little smirk on his face, began to peddle just a little faster. Smirking back, I went past him. The other two moved up. It was like a food fight, when you've got a little ketchup on your finger and you flip it at a guy, then he deliberately puts mustard on his and flips it at you. Before any of us knew it, we were bombing down Port Crescent as fast as we could go. We peddled crazily on our Schwinns, big, heavy bikes without gears. When we got to where Port Crescent intersected Huron, I saw a chance to take the lead and cut through the driveway and gas pumps at Jim's Pure, tilting into the turn, yelling and shrieking. A couple of Jim's customers scattered to get out of the way. One man nearly climbed his car; another dived into Jim's doorway.

For a few seconds I was swollen with power, intoxicated with my own craziness. The other guys whooped and yelled behind me.

Huron Lanes is next to Jim's Pure, and I think if we'd come straight down Huron, Clara might have seen us, but because we cut the corner, we were invisible to her. The car door opened, Clara got out, and I hit her. We flew, like one congealed mass, into the door, which strained to come off its hinges. There we hung for a long moment, until the car door pushed back. The handlebars wrenched and spun from my hands. I caught the end of one in my gut as the bike came out from under me, and we crashed in a heap. I landed under Clara and the bike. I tried to pull myself out from under, but I was caught. Then Clara started to sob.

People in the bowling alley slowly realized there'd been an accident. Al came out, trying to help Clara get up. I was trying to catch my breath. Somebody pulled me out from under the bike. Al started to cry along with Clara. Before they got her in the car to go to Hubbard Hospital, Al looked at me, halfway between accusation and concern, tears running down his cheeks, and said, "Doug are you OK? Did you get hurt?" I couldn't speak. I just shook my head. I had been standing there, holding my side, watching Clara crying. Somebody pulled his station wagon around to Clara, and Al tenderly helped her into the backseat. Al's "Doug, are you OK? Did you get hurt?" echoed in my brain. God.

Clara had cried harder when she moved to the car.

My bike was unridable. The front wheel was twisted. It takes a hell of an impact to do that to a Schwinn. I left the bike at the gas station, and Jim gave me a ride home, where I told my parents what I'd done to two of their best friends. They went straight to the hospital. I went upstairs and cried. Clara had two cracked ribs and a knee that might have been clipped by a pro football player. Her left side was one big bruise. When Dad came home, he found me upstairs, just past the blubbering stage. He put his hand on my shoulder and said, "Doug, I don't know what gets into you sometimes. Jim told me you nearly mowed down two of his customers before you hit Clara."

"How is she?"

"She's still crying, the poor thing."

I went with my parents to see Clara in the hospital. She had a black eye, her side hurt, and she groaned when the nurses tried to get her out of bed. Al was there when we visited. I could barely look him or Clara in the eye. I said I was sorry. Really, really, sorry.

I thought I'd wrecked my Dad's friendship with Al, but Al was more decent than that, and so was my dad. I stayed out of the bowling alley and cringed when I had to walk past its big windows. Whenever I saw Clara, limping the short distance from her car to a store or the bowling alley, I wished my body would unravel, atom by atom.

Larry Horgan leaves the Bad Axe Theater with tears in his eyes. He is still hearing, "There's a place for us. . . ." *West Side Story* is

the most beautiful thing he has ever seen. Natalie Wood leaves a
hollow ache in his gut. He will sneak to the movies many more
times before he finally gets caught, and then he will turn his back
on his father's church, even though he will still have to go, every
Sunday, until he leaves for college. *West Side Story* will break the
first part of his life away from what follows, the way a dead twig
can be snapped from a tree.

When Larry comes out the theater door, the work of three
hours' heavy snowfall lies before him. The steps to the theater are
pristine, buried in loose snow. The whole city is wrapped in it.
Only in the streets, where a few cars have passed, is the white layer marred. Parking meters wear white caps and stick up from the
sidewalk like a rank of frozen old men. The town's only stoplight,
three blocks away, fills the streets with green, then red. Larry
holds his breath. His tears freeze to his cheeks, and he decides to
walk home along the backstreets, which are even quieter and
more mysterious than what he sees before him.

After Chino shoots Tony dead, before Dad gets to his eighth
frame, I am mostly buried. I watch the snow come down, like a
hazy mass of starfall, hear the flakes bumping into each other,
making chords and chimes like bowling balls hitting pins, only
faint, faint. I am surprised I've never heard them before. For me,
that night, the chime of colliding snowflakes becomes the sound
of Bad Axe. The snow doesn't so much pile onto me as I sink into
it. The light from Clara McLean's window falls aslant my legs. I
tell myself to get up, but lying there, listening to the snow, is so
pleasant that I lose the will to move. My foot sticks up impudently
on the old, frozen snow, and a little breeze swirls, keeping it from
getting covered. I think I'd be more comfortable if someone
would come along and pull the white blanket over my foot, but
doing it myself is too much trouble. The snow covers my eyes.

Larry walks down Hanselman Street, sticking his tongue out to
catch snowflakes. He wouldn't do such a childish thing if anyone
were in the streets. It is wonderful to be alone in a snow-filled city.

Maybe, Larry thinks, school will be canceled tomorrow. He zigs up and down the side streets, in no hurry to be home. His parents will have to drive very slowly on the way back from the airport, and even if they beat him home, he'll just say he'd been out for a walk. Which will be true!

Larry goes past the McLeans' house and glimpses something odd out of the corner of his eye. He keeps walking for half a block, until what he has seen develops in his mind like a Polaroid going from cloudy to clear. A shoe sticking out of the snow. He turns around slowly and walks back to the McLeans' yard. Then he runs. He grabs my shoe and starts dusting the snow away, discovering the blue jeans connected to the shoe. He brushes snow away as fast as he can, working his way up, until he is smacking my nose back and forth.

"Doug!" He shakes me. "Doug! Are you OK? Wake up!" He bounces me around. I can sort of feel it.

He grabs me under the arms, pulls me across the lawn, onto the sidewalk, and up the McLeans' steps. My feet go thunk, thunk all the way up. Larry rings the McLeans' doorbell, again and again, then pounds on the door. It opens, and light floods the porch. Clara is in a housecoat, clutching it around her, trying to keep warm.

"It's Doug O'Dell, Mrs. McLean. I found him in your yard. I think he's frozen."

Dad is in the ninth frame. The other games have almost stopped. People in the bowling alley are straining to see what is going to happen on alley three. When Dad makes the strike, a huge cheer goes up. Al McLean is not only smoking his cigar, but chewing it as well. So much smoke is going up he might as well be a train engine. When Dad gets to the tenth frame, a hush settles over the place, the kind of hush that can only be accentuated by an announcer's whisper, like on *Big Time Bowling,* when Ray Blooth goes to the line.

The woman who tends the pop bar tugs on Al's sleeve.

"Not now," he grumbles.

She pulls again and whispers something in his ear. He goes to the phone and drops his cigar.

Dad goes into his five-step approach dance and releases the ball. He's so smooth tonight, you can't even hear the ball hit the alley. It's heading for the pocket and everyone knows it's another strike. Down comes the pinsetter to clear away the debris. Dad waits for the ball to return.

Al, who no one has ever seen hurry, except for the time I ran into Clara, shoulders his way through the crowd, grabs Dad by the arm, and whispers in his ear. The ball comes back. The pins are set up. Does my father look wistfully at the pins, the crowd, his hand, which ought to fit into that ball?

He is heading for the door as fast as he can with Al hot behind him.

Larry drags me inside. Clara soaks a bath towel with warm water and slaps it on my chest. I go from numb to freezing. Dad and Al arrive. Larry and Dad toss me into the backseat of Dad's car like a Yule log and take me to the hospital. I want to say something, but my jaw feels rusted shut. Nurses strip me and put me into a big tub of hot water. I am not so frozen that I can't be embarrassed. When I start to shiver, I think I will shake myself to pieces. I can't stop.

Early the next morning, my father and mother and Clara and Al come to the hospital. Clara puts her hand on my cheek and leaves it there, as if touch could heal. It is an old, very soft hand, and against the light on the ceiling Clara looks like a wrinkled, white-haired angel, engulfed in halo. "Doug, you gave me such a scare."

"I'm sorry," I croak. "I'm sorry." She smiles softly at me. "I know," she says.

Later, Larry shows up. He tells me, "If I hadn't sinned and gone to see *West Side Story*, you'd be dead."

At Jim's Pure, for the next week or so, people will debate these events. Did the alcohol in my veins keep me alive, like antifreeze, or nearly kill me, like the doctor said, because it shut down my shivering response? The antifreeze theory will be popular at Jim's. Would Dad have made those last two strikes? Some will say, yes, he was in the groove, but others will argue that under the mounting pressure of ten straight strikes, he would have been more likely to falter. They will debate more heatedly over whether Dad should have stayed and bowled those last two balls, or whether Al McLean should have said anything about me until after the game. I will be labeled a royal pain in the ass by the whole town. And what about my father? they'll say. He was so close, he'll wonder for the rest of his life whether he could have bowled a perfect game. What should he do with a kid like me?

I feel bad, of course. But for the first time since I hit Clara McLean, I feel better.

THE MESSAGE BOARD

When you get to be seventy-five years old and your dad's pushing ninety-six, it gets kind of hard to keep the father/son relationship straight. I remember Dad telling me, when he was around my age, that each extra day was gravy, that hell, he'd never counted on living *this* long. His father'd died of a heart attack at fifty-eight, and it hadn't stopped Dad from smoking and drinking and eating chicken-fried steak, just as it hasn't stopped me. Trouble was, Dad found out, each day after eighty-five was a helluva pain in the ass. "Triple bypass, gall bladder removed, skin cancers scraped off m' face, no teeth, eyes damn near gone—macular fucking degeneration—hearing aids screwed into both m' damn ears, can't taste nothin', got the shakes. Shit Billy, just cash it in by the time you're eighty-five." One contemporary to another.

"I'll try to time it," I said. In the old folks home, the high thermostat setting used to get to me, but these days, it feels pretty comfortable. What's frustrated Dad the most over the last few years is that he can't read. Oh, he can make out a word or two with his glasses on, if he holds a big-print book up to his nose, but there's no joy in reading one word at a time, and he hasn't got the stamina to get far with it. This is hard on him in other ways, because Mom was an English teacher, and we all just got into the comfortable habit of reading. I think the whole Missoula Public Library went through our house piecemeal when I was a kid, ex-

cept for the encyclopedia and the dictionary, which didn't circu-
late. I read everybody from Edgar Rice Burroughs to Plato, and
although since then there've been big stretches of my life when I
haven't read, there've been other big stretches when I've done little else. Now, I'm limited to four or five hours a day, spread out,
because my eyes get tired.

Before she died, about ten years ago, my mother did a remark-
able thing. She had cancer and knew the end wasn't far off, so
she started reading poetry into a cassette tape recorder: Shakespeare's *Sonnets* took up three cassettes; Donne and Herbert got
a cassette each. She liked Renaissance poets—Gascoigne, Sidney,
Wyatt, Ralegh, Fulke Greville—and she put a miscellaneous assortment of them on another tape. Then she died.

Dad and I passed those tapes back and forth for several years,
listening to Mom's voice, reedy but sweet, and very exact. We'd
have worn those tapes out, but we got smart after awhile and
made duplicates. It's like a piece of Mom is still alive, and I know
this is a comfort to Dad. I've listened to the tapes so many times
I've picked up a good many of those poems by heart. I get him
other tapes from the public library, and sometimes I even buy
tapes that we share, like the entire *Odyssey,* read by Ian McKellan.
Takes over thirteen hours to listen to the whole thing, but hell,
that poem was meant to be listened to. In the winter, in front of
the fireplace, you can pretend you're a Greek, twenty-five hundred years ago, listening to Homer. But no matter how many
tapes I dig up, it's Mom reading the *Sonnets* that I love best.

We were listening to a new one, Kenneth Branagh doing *Ham-
let,* and I was watching the snow falling thicker and thicker outside Dad's window. At 5:00, halfway through act 2, I decided I'd
better go. We shook hands, and Dad said, "Billy, you be careful
out there." I got on the road home just as the blizzard was kick-
ing up. I put in Mom's sonnet tape, and her voice sounded in the
pickup like a piece of the wind. The snow came down in big flakes
that got smaller as the wind blew harder. By the time Mom got to
Sonnet 22, I was thinking, I'll have to use the chains and crawl
home; my fingers stiffened at the idea of wrestling with cold met-

al in drifting snow. Pretty soon, the snow was blowing crossways through the high beams so thick, all I could see were two staticky snow cones stretching out ahead of me. I had been on the road an hour, and I doubt I had covered thirty miles. Mom was getting to Sonnet 73, "That time of year thou mayest in me behold / When yellow leaves, or none, or few, do hang," and that's when I saw the guy, right in front of me, walking like a ghost down the middle of my lane. His back was to me, and his head was pulled turtle fashion into his shoulders. I hit the brakes, jerked the steering wheel to the left, and, whoosh, the truck started doing donuts. I thought, *Damn it, that's it for the night,* but when the world stopped spinning around, I was still on the road, facing backwards, and the guy was trudging towards me, through the little drifts, like nothing had happened. I paused a second, stunned by the odds. He had loafers on and a windbreaker, snow caked all over him. He knocked politely on the cab window and said, "C-c-c-can I come in?"

I was tempted to ask him whether he was trying to get the both of us killed, but he looked damn near killed already, so I cracked the window and just said, "Get in." I turned off the tape, got the pickup pointed around the right way, went out and put the chains on, my finger joints damn near seizing up on me. By the time I got back in, he didn't even look like he'd started to thaw, so I hauled out the sleeping bag from behind my seat and tucked it up around him.

After we got down the road a ways, I just couldn't help myself, and I said, "What the hell were you doing back there, trying to get yourself killed?"

His teeth were chattering like a bunch of balls in an electric bingo machine. "Car went off the road," he croaked, "looking for a gas station."

"Nearest would be Red Path," I said. "They've got a truck stop up there. Probably packed by now. We're going to have to stop and wait this one out. I just hope we get that far."

We did. Got lucky and followed a snowplow all the way in. By then the truck stop looked like an outpost on some volatile outer planet. The place was nearly full, and would get overfull as the night went on. Stranded truckers, ranchers, small-town businessmen. The hardy people of Montana know a losing proposition when they see one. The only rational response to this storm was patience. Sit tight and let 'er blow. I knew a few of these people, tipped my hat and said hi. I knew the owner, Marlene, from way back. She liked these blizzards. Made her feel like some frontier version of the Red Cross, preserving the community.

The guy and I climbed into the last booth, and Marlene brought over a pot of coffee. "Hi Billy," she said. "What catches you out in all this?"

"Over visiting Dad."

"How's the old coot doin'?"

"His body's too stubborn to give out on him."

"Probably make a hundred."

I nodded. "Whether he wants to or not."

The guy was pouring down cup after cup of coffee loaded with sugar, thawing from the inside out. I had a few cups myself, then I just waited, wondering if he was going to talk.

I don't pry into other people's lives, but there we were, stuck at Marlene's with about forty other people, nothing to do but stare at each other until dawn. Nobody was going to get any sleep. It takes a mighty reticent man to keep his mouth shut in a situation like that. Marlene scared up a couple decks of cards, and a few games got going, but that didn't occupy us. We had some vegetable soup, and I think we were both feeling pretty glad to be inside.

"How'd you go off the road?" I asked, trying to get things started.

The man eyed me for a while. Then he said, "I got scared. The way the snow was going through the headlights, moving so fast, and so much of it. The beam solid with moving snow. It reminded me of something." He shivered. "I just spun off the road and got stuck. I used to live in Fresno," he said. "Snow free. I really don't know how to drive in it."

I nodded.

"But now I live toward Kalispell. Got a little cabin up there this summer. Are you married?" he said, looking at my left hand.

"Wife passed on. Got kids and grandkids in Denver and Seattle." I told him about my family, about what it was like to look for oil and to have a ranch in Montana. Some people like to talk about themselves, but I like to listen. Still, you got to prime the pump sometimes with the quiet ones, talk about yourself to get something back. I finished with a story about one of my granddaughters.

"That's nice," he said. "I had a family." He stared out the window for a while at the white chaos.

I didn't push him, but little by little, his conversational drip turned into a nice smooth flow and then a gusher. The guy said his name was James Kelsey, and I just let him talk. He looked a little wild: red-rimmed eyelids, long, thinned-out hair. He had a gurgly voice—coming down with a cold, I suppose—but his story came out in a careful and erudite mass, like he'd written it out and memorized it, or rehearsed it in his brain, over and over again, like he was listening to a cassette tape:

"Everything that's happened to me in the last three years comes from a dream," he said. "In September and October, I used to go stargazing at Big Stump—that's in Kings Canyon National Park—with my family, but mainly with my daughter Alice. Sheila and John were good for one night of star watching, and then they wanted to snuggle into a nice warm cabin. But Ali loved the Milky Way. We'd go up to the national park for a couple weekends each fall, rent a cabin, and get away from the air pollution in Fresno. I could feel the tension drain away from me with each thousand-foot gain in elevation. By the six-thousand-foot mark we'd be in the park at Grant Grove, where the air smelled of cedar and redwood and damp ground.

"Most people have never seen the Milky Way. They live in cities that light up the sky and blot out all but the brightest stars. Even in rural areas with good air and little light, the Milky Way usually appears as a faint smear of stars, barely perceptible as a whole.

You sure can't see it from Fresno or anywhere else in the smoggy San Joaquin Valley. To really see it, you have to gain altitude. Six thousand feet is enough. In the parking lot at Big Stump, straight overhead, the Milky Way is a grainy mass of individual stars, like sequins on a black gown. Each star is too small to utterly distinguish it from its neighbors, yet many are too hard and bright to be lost in a general blur.

"The Milky Way goes from north to south. In the south, it does become a blur, because that's the area where the galactic core lies, the star-crammed furnace that our sun orbits every several million years. I like the view straight up, held until your neck gets stiff, vertigo takes hold, and you feel yourself plunging into the sky. This scenario forms part of the dream I'm going to tell you about, the beginning of it, but it doesn't quite convey the feel of the dream or the reality, so I need to go back and tell you about something else.

"Every time I went to Big Stump, I was surprised to have my sense of direction contradicted by the position of the stars. I have a good sense of direction, I think, and I tend to know where I am in the woods, even on circuitous trails. But the road from Grant Grove to Big Stump always confused me. At Grant Grove, you point your car west, and north is where it ought to be, on your right. The road twists and turns, and by the time you get to Big Stump, only a few minutes away, you are apparently pointed east with the south on your right. This hundred-eighty-degree twist never registers on my directional sense. I turn into the parking lot, and I get out of the car convinced at an intuitive level that Polaris will be low in the sky, on my right, on the far side of the parking lot I feel to be north. Instead, it hangs on the left, over the entrance to the parking lot, and the sense never leaves me that it's just all wrong. Even as the night progresses, and as many times as I've done this, my intuitive conviction refuses to align itself with absolute evidence.

"My dream starts at the message board at Grant Grove. It's by the grocery store. People coming up to go camping leave messages for each other, like, 'Kim, Left Azalea Campground and have gone on to Cedar Grove, Marty.' I'm there at the message board, convinced that someone's left a message for me, but I can't find it. I get quite frustrated. I know it's up there, but the board is plastered with messages, and I can't find the one that's meant for me. I know it's important, but I don't know why. When my frustration is about to peak, I find myself at Big Stump, late at night, with Ali.

"Big Stump is the same as always except for a couple things. The first incongruity is that I do *not* have the usual feeling of incongruity about direction. The North Star is exactly where I would *like* it to be and, therefore, exactly on the wrong side of the parking lot. It taunts me, because although now intuition and evidence have embraced like sweethearts, what about all those other times? Now, doubt about my memory plagues me. The universe is not supposed to line itself up with our preferences. I've always found the dependability of that comforting. It means I haven't duped myself into some happy fantasy. It means truth and objectivity still exist.

"I stand in the parking lot, oohing and aahing with Ali, staring straight up into the Great Rift, that long jagged black canyon in the middle of the Milky Way. The Rift narrows on either end, and the Milky Way closes again, at both ends of the rift, becoming a solid band of stars. Astronomy books offer the explanation that the Rift is a giant gas cloud that interposes itself between us and our view of the galaxy, blocking out those micrograined stars as if they were not even there. But just looking up, it seems that the Milky Way has been ripped apart, creating a black gulf in the middle of the ribbon.

"As I stare at the Rift, the location changes. I am no longer in the parking lot with Ali but by myself, at a much higher elevation, on the top of a granite dome. The wind is cold, and the few pine trees that cling to life in the cracks of the rock are dwarfish and blasted. It reminds me of Little Baldy or Half Dome, but the altitude is much higher, and I am shivering from cold. The stars themselves, as if part of some vast refrigeration unit, are bigger, brighter, sharper against the eye. I could rub my hands along the Milky Way as if it were sandpaper, stick my hand into the Great Rift and cut my fingers on its serrated edges. Here, with no trees in the way, stars cover the night sky from horizon to horizon.

"I begin to realize that I have to find my way off the top of this dome in the dark, or perhaps die of hypothermia. Then I hear a great detonation, the sound of ice breaking from the polar caps, but deeper, more resonant, and with such release of energy, the rock beneath me vibrates. Within the Great Rift, the sky is coming apart, as if someone has pulled a knife across the belly of the night and eviscerated it. Through the Rift, at first, stars fall like flour from a sifter, and as the rip widens, a deluge of stars, like snowflakes in a blizzard, fall, swirling, eating up the night in a cloud of stellar confusion.

"The sky disintegrates. Stars drift to the ground as white ash. I'm up to my ankles in it, up to my knees; the color of the sky is no longer blue or black but merely . . . lit up. Light without color. What I am seeing is the end of the universe. It is not Judgment Day. No Jesus coming out of the sky on a white horse followed by legions of angels. No rapture, no people standing in open graves, waiting to be judged. The universe, and everything that makes it cohere, has simply failed. The rock on which I stand begins to bust up. Atomic bonds relax. I look down and see myself beginning to effervesce, and as if spirit has been set loose from matter, billions of homeless dwindling souls moan.

"Which is when I always woke up screaming, Sheila holding me, telling me how hard I had been trying to wake up, to escape from the grip of the dream. I couldn't go back to sleep after that. I got out of bed, went to the kitchen, and Sheila, pale under the kitchen light, drank chamomile tea with me as I tried to calm down, telling her the dream from start to finish. I had the dream twice more that night, each time exactly the same, and each time, I woke up in the same state, sweating and yelling, Sheila looking at me big-eyed, her mouth out of Edvard Munch.

"Sheila got the kids off to school the next morning and dragged herself off to work. 'Maybe you should see a doctor,' she said. I didn't know what to say to that. She was clearly frightened—frightened not only for me, but of me, a little bit. I doubted my GP would have had anything constructive to say. I could hear it now: working too hard, take it easy, maybe a few days off. In fact, I'd come to that decision myself. I was in no shape to go to work. I was in no shape for anything. I didn't want to eat. After all, I'd watched my hand turn into a cloud of subatomic particles. The mountain, the ash, had bubbled away like Alka-Seltzer. And this had happened three times, in exactly the same way. That's what really got to me. I could think of nothing but the dream.

"Now, I'm not a flake. I'm not big on dream interpretation. From what I've read, dreams could as well be the random by-products of chemoelectric activity as Freud's elaborate tales of the subconscious. Psychology has never impressed me. But I now thought of going to a psychiatrist, or even a priest, because the same dream just doesn't occur three times a night, does it? Not in the exact same way. But I didn't seek help, not yet. I spent the day stretched out on the La-Z-Boy recliner in my den, staring at the spines of my books.

"What can I say about the next six days and nights, except that it got worse? On the second night, I looked forward to a long, sound sleep, but the dream repeated itself again, three times, and each time it got clearer. I didn't get used to it. If anything, it disturbed me more and more. Each time, I thrashed Sheila out of her sleep, and she got up with me until exhaustion took us off again. Tuesday morning, we could barely get out of bed, but she got the kids to school, and I forced myself to go to work. I was in the wills and trusts section of the biggest law firm in Fresno. In wills and trusts, taxation, corporate and business law, we are not given to enthusiasm, and if we have strange imaginings, we keep them to ourselves. I didn't tell a soul. But I couldn't work. I was too tired, and trusts had grown to seem—not boring, they'd always been that—but stupid, beside the point, though what the "point" was, I didn't know. The third night, between dreams, Sheila and I sat at the kitchen table, looking at each other out of our sunken eyes like a pair of drunken raccoons. 'Tomorrow night I'm going to sleep in the guest room,' I said. There was no argument.

"What I mean by the dreams getting clearer, I think, is that my senses were being sharpened. We go through life pretty much dead to our surroundings, the captives of routine. That, of course, is axiomatic, clichéd—but true. The opposite was happening to me. I was being treated to a routine to which I became more and more alert. Now the brightness of the stars felt like pinpricks on my cheeks. The crystals in the granite dome stood out with their own topography: huge hunks of feldspar, ice fields of quartz, great table-lands of mica. In the parking lot, Ali's body glowed and threw off heat like a furnace, and as everything became more real, the obliteration of it all at the end became harder to bear. Just losing one star, one crystal from the granite on which I stood, seemed like a universe of tragedies. On the fourth night, instead of waking up screaming, I woke up crying.

"The next day I decided I wouldn't go to sleep. I would sit up and watch TV all night. I had called in sick on the third and fourth days, and by then, I *was* getting sick. My throat was raspy. My sinuses drained down my throat. I needed sleep, but I didn't need the dream. I went to Starbucks, bought a coffee press and a pound of espresso beans. That night I turned on *Letterman* and started sipping caffeine. I probably nodded off around midnight. When the dream awoke me, I started drinking coffee again. When I awoke from the third and last dream, around 6:00 in the morning, I had a hell of a caffeine buzz. By Sunday, after the last of the dreams, I was just a bit insane, and Sheila wasn't far behind. The children watched me with big eyes and did not say a word. Sunday night, the dream did not come.

"I spent the next month in terror that the dream would come back. Then the next, and the next, until finally, exhausted, having missed so much work my job was in jeopardy, I realized the dream was through with me, and I had only to wonder what it meant. So I tried to resume life as usual, my lucrative, humdrum, pleasantly boring life. But I couldn't. The dream had taken most of me with it. The world was such a pale shadow of the dream that it didn't hold my attention, and the dream had raised all the questions that are so inconvenient to a man trying to earn a lot of money—like, 'Why bother?' I'd sit in the recliner, looking around the living room, thinking everything I owned, everything I'd done, was insubstantial crap. I went to the office, stared at trust files, and could not work on them. I couldn't even open them. This paralysis at the office went on for weeks, months. Fewer files came my way. The partners were discreetly rerouting clients; people I'd brought to the firm were slowly being taken away from me, and it was a good thing, because I was nothing like a competent lawyer anymore. Nothing that lawyers did, nor any kind of other effort, seemed worthwhile. I lost forty pounds before I regained a minimal interest in eating.

"Finally the day came when Matt Carlyle, the managing partner, had to tell me I was through. He was very kind, very discreet, and started with a long preamble about how valuable I'd been to the firm.

'Jim,' he said, 'have you looked into getting some help?'

"I didn't pretend not to know what he was talking about. I just said, 'No.'

'Would you like to take a leave for a while, try to pull yourself together? We know something happened to you about a year ago. Some of us think you had a nervous breakdown—that you still haven't recovered.'

"Matt really was trying to be helpful. He was a genuinely decent human being. The crow's feet around his eyes deepened as he looked at me. I tried to feel as concerned about myself as he did, but it was no go.

'I'll tell you what, Jim. I want you to take some time. Six months. Even take a year. We'll carry you for that long. Your draw from the firm will be reduced somewhat, but you'll still be OK. I'm sure, given some time, you'll feel like yourself again. Meanwhile,' he gave me a card, 'I want you to see this guy. After Dorothy and I broke up he did me a world of good.'

"The card said, 'William Ellis, Psychologist.'

'OK, Matt,' I said.

'We'll cover your clients.'

'I know you will. You've been doing it for nearly a year now,' I said tiredly.

'Well, you just get better. Enjoy yourself. Get away from the stress.'

'Right. Thanks Matt. You've been great. Everybody's been great. I'm sorry I've let you down.'

'You haven't let us down. Don't even think about it.'

"He ushered me out the door of the firm. I think we both knew I'd never be back.

"Sheila and I went on an 'austerity' budget—still enough to make payments on our $400,000 house and live comfortably besides, but only for a year. Sheila kept urging me to see the psychologist, and I finally did. I'd been trying to do some research on the dream—Freud, Jung—I'd read Revelations half a dozen times.

"The psychologist didn't seem all that interested in my dream, though he did want to know everything else. How was my libido? *Just fine,* I said. He smiled approvingly.

'Good, regular sexual relations would tend to indicate you are not depressed.'

'Who said anything about regular sex?'

'You said your libido was just fine,' he said.

'It is.'

'But you just implied you don't engage in sex very frequently.'

'I haven't engaged in it at all—not for over a year.'

'But . . . I don't understand.'

'I don't miss it. My libido is relaxed. Relaxed to the max.'

"He scribbled a few notes. We went over my relationship with the kids, which I described as low-energy unconditional love.

'Maybe we should have your wife come to one of these sessions,' he said, brow furrowed.

"I shrugged. 'Fine with me.'

"He was getting irked too, just as Sheila had finally become irked. As the session hit one conversational cul-de-sac after another, he finally dropped his approach and said, 'OK, tell me about your dream.'

"I did. 'What do you make of it?' I asked.

'What do *you* make of it?' he responded.

'I'm not inclined to go into allegory or symbolism. I think the dream is exactly what it seems to be: an utterly nihilistic vision. The universe is insubstantial, something concocted by the Wizard of Oz that finally comes apart at the seams. The trouble is there's no wizard, no machine. That's what really bothers me, because it's at odds with the way I received the dream. The idea that the world we perceive is just a blind for a more real world—that's Christian, Platonic, Hindu. But my dream shows no more real world behind this one. In my dream the universe is revealed as pure fairy dust, Maya—no Jesus behind it, no Brahma, no nothing. But then I think of the way I got the dream. Three per night, seven straight nights. There's nothing nihilistic about that. The number seven comes up time after time in Revelations. There are seven deadly sins, seven virtues, seven days in a week. Three is the trinity. I had twenty-one dreams total. The trinity times seven is twenty-one. Or just say to hell with numerological tie-ins altogether. Those dreams happened at the same time of the night, three times a night, for seven days in a row, exactly the same way—there's order there, not nihilism. The content of the dream does not jibe with the orderliness of the delivery system, and why the same dream again and again?' Here, I'm afraid, I started to get a little excited. 'What am I? Something to torture? Some kind of fucking cosmic message board? I mean, what happened? Is somebody or something trying to communicate with me? Was I on the receiving end of some cosmic information leak, some spillage from the night sky where the sutures of time and space suddenly gave way? And why *me*? I mean, *what the fuck goes on here?*'

"By this time the psychologist thought he had a prize nutcase in hand, publication material: 'I think we'd better start out with twice a week. How are Tuesday and Thursday afternoons?'

"I walked out of the psychologist's office shivering. Maybe I *was* going fucking nuts. You see, I hadn't realized until the discussion with the psychologist just how angry I was. I'd had a nice, if blinkered, life. I'd done all the things that a good father and husband was supposed to do. Made lots of money. Made my family the center of my life outside of work. Hadn't drunk. Hadn't chased women. I was free of the obsessions that plague most people and thankful for it. And I wasn't smug or complacent either. Like any good bourgeois lawyer, I was smart enough to know that things could be taken away from people in ways they couldn't anticipate, couldn't defend against. But by a dream? It was as if some malevolent deity, who relentlessly refused to show himself, had wreaked vengeance on me for my quiet good fortune, had thrown something at me with such force that it was now twisted up with my very DNA. I wanted the dream to speak to me, explain itself in some kind of comfortable epilogue, where a white-bearded man in coveralls sits down with me in some mountain cabin and explains step by step just what it's about. I wait for such a dream, for my Zen master to come down from Cold Mountain. It's been over three years, I've been through a divorce, and I've never had that epilogue. I suppose I never will.

"Sheila stuck it out six months longer, then took the kids, moved back east, and got a divorce in Ohio. I didn't take the trouble to hire a lawyer. I had inherited a little money that Sheila let me keep. I've been living on that. I haven't really worked since that twenty-first dream. Maybe I'm crazy. But I do not walk down the street, talking and gesturing urgently to myself or some unseen listener. I do not sleep on steam gratings or dine out of dumpsters. As far as I can tell, I am not the victim of hallucinations, visual, auditory, or olfactory. But I am the victim of dreams, the same dream, that I had over and over again, all night long, for seven nights in a row, each time experiencing it as newer than the time before, as if each iteration of the dream just peeled away another layer of me until there were no more left to peel, until by the morning after the seventh night I was a man flayed to the bone by dream, polished by it. What would a psychologist know about that?"

◆

By this time it was about 4:00 in the morning. People were getting dopey, but they weren't falling asleep, except maybe for a couple with their heads down on their tables.

"So what now?" I said. "Just thinking about your dream all that time?"

"Yeah. That's about it."

"Traveling around the country like the Ancient Mariner, stopping wedding guests?"

He looked at me queerly. Didn't expect an old geezer with a cowboy hat and a fifteen-year-old pickup truck to be literate.

"You think I'm a nut," he said. "Somebody who goes around accosting people with a ridiculous story."

"No, I don't."

"I haven't told anyone about this since—since the psychologist."

"OK. It just seems to me you're forgetting something."

"What."

"Everything you said about how Polaris was on the wrong side of the parking lot and how you liked a universe that didn't give way to solipsism."

He looked at me.

"Yeah, I know what the word means," I said. "Look. Polaris turns up on the wrong side of the parking lot. Then the universe disintegrates. Maybe you're just telling yourself that any world in which Polaris is in the south would be a sham—would be just a product of your imagination, and subject to disintegration. The world of your dream is that kind of a nightmare. But it's not the way the world really is."

He looked at me as if I were a hobgoblin. "You mean, you think my dream's just an argument? Just a demonstration that a solipsistic world can't hold together?"

"Why not?"

"You're suggesting that I've let something that banal ruin my life?"

"Maybe you wanted your life to change. I'd think being a trust lawyer could seem pretty artificial at times. And family life can be stultifying." I'm a hell of an amateur psychologist. It's easier than playing a good game of chess, though I do play good chess, over the Internet, couple, three times a week and also in Missoula at the Big Sky Chess Club.

"Hey, but wait a minute. Why all the dreams? Why would I have such a stupid dream three dreams in a night, seven nights in a row? Come on!"

"Maybe you're stubborn," I said, "maybe you hate to listen to yourself."

"But that message didn't *need* to get through. If you're right about what the dream means, it already gibed with what I consciously thought. That solipsism is stupid wasn't any deep dark secret bubbling up from my unconscious."

"I don't know," I said. "Is there an unconscious? Maybe we dream about our conscious concerns. Maybe the dream is just the message that you wanted to find so much at the message board by the grocery store: that real and imaginary worlds behave in different ways, that the real world exists independently of our dreams about it. Or maybe it's simpler yet: the lack of message at the message board was just a way to tell you, ahead of time, that the dream had no message. Or maybe the dreams just gave you an excuse to throw over your life. Maybe you wanted disruption."

"That's absurd," the guy said, but he sounded a little shocked. "I haven't seen my children in three years," he muttered.

I just shook my head. He'd let something loose in me, something that got the better of my manners. We didn't have much to say to each other after that. He folded his arms on the table and put his head down, but I don't think he slept. I think he was looking at the formica, close range.

By morning the snowplows had done a pretty good job of opening the roads, the storm was letting up a little, and many of the people at Marlene's, especially the truckers, began to drift out. I went to the men's room—Marlene's coffee had been sending me there regularly all night—and when I got back to the booth, the guy was gone. "Took off with one of the truckers," Marlene said. "But he put something up for you on the message board."

I walked over to the bulletin board, mostly filled with cards for local businesses in Missoula, a few in Kalispell, Red Path. Truckers used to use the board, but now, what with radios and cell phones, they don't much. There was a napkin up there, tacked to the board; ink had soaked in and made the guy's letters big and fuzzy. "I hope it happens to you someday," it said. "Jim." Car keys hung from the tack. "It's yours," the note ended.

I gave the car keys to Marlene. "Why don't you call the state patrol. Tell 'em these are from an abandoned car. Probably on 93 somewhere. If they want to know anything about it, tell 'em to call me."

I went home. My neighbor, Jerry Gaither, had plowed out the long road down to the house, so I got in without getting stuck. At my age, it's good to have dependable people like Jerry close by. That night, I put on my parka and looked at the stars. I went out in the snow and laid on my back, under the dark kitchen window, just staring straight up. Hadn't done that in a long, long time. No trouble seeing the Milky Way, bright and grainy, just like the guy said. There's always a moment looking up, when the sky goes from two dimensions to three, and the stars open up just like you'd put on stereoscopic glasses. The guy's right, I thought: it didn't look solid, and according to quantum mechanics, it was possible for matter to do crazy things. It was possible, though highly improbable, for the air molecules in an auditorium to all go whizzing to one corner, and leave the audience gasping. I supposed it was possible for the universe to do much the same thing. The stars shimmered, perhaps contemplating anarchy. I could hear my mother's voice in the gusting wind, finishing Sonnet 73.

CENTER OF GRAVITY

Schmidt was forty-eight, and he was wearing out. He could no longer tell the difference between his good knee and his bad knee, and it was weird: one of his toes—that long one on the right foot—hurt at the joints. A toe, for crying out loud. He, who had struggled to the top of Half Dome the summer before, no longer had the energy for evening walks. His bones rebelled. For the last couple of years, he'd had to hold the newspaper at half an arm's length to read it. Now, he'd gone to a full arm's length, and truth be told, he read the back page most comfortably when Renee held up the paper, reading to herself on the other side of the table.

And his hearing was going. One Sunday morning, he was at the kitchen table, having coffee with Renee, when she said thoughtfully, "I think I need a mastodon."

"What?" he said, at first thinking she might be referring to sex, somehow.

She looked at him languidly, coffee cup poised.

"A mastodon? You think you need a mastodon?"

"I said," she replied, enunciating very carefully, "'I think I must have done it wrong.' The crossword." She waved her section of the *Detroit Free Press* at him. "I'm going to test your hearing," she said. "You've been sounding just like my patients."

"You need to speak up. You mumble."

"That's what they all say. 'I can hear just fine. If only my wife would stop mumbling.'"

"Well, in some cases it must be true."

She shook her head. Eyes, ears, joints. Who knew what would go next?

His patience had apparently worn out at the same rate as his cartilage. Each day on the way to the university, weaving through the Ann Arbor traffic, there was always one driver he wanted to throttle, and sometimes a half-dozen. It was the same on the way home. He was off-kilter, suffering from some kind of erosion at the core, and it spun him in odd directions. He loved his kids more with each passing year, and yet, part of him wished they'd grow up, leave home, and move into a dorm, because they'd become even sloppier as teenagers than they had been when they were little. He felt like yelling at them all the time, but it never helped anything.

For instance, Schmidt had decided it was his duty as a father to get upset about his son's lousy grades. After all, Schmidt's father had gotten upset with him, plenty, and eventually, Schmidt had responded. It dawned on him, one night when he was in sixth grade, that he really wanted to make his father proud of him, and from then on, he put everything he had into excelling in school and atheletics. Schmidt thought it would work the same for Jerry. He was afraid that if he didn't rant a little, Jerry might think it was OK to keep getting D's and comments like "doesn't hand in homework," "could try harder," and "comes to class unprepared."

Schmidt tried to be a method actor when it came to fatherly performances, working up to them. When the storms broke, usually a couple of days after Jerry brought home his report card, the poor kid never knew what hit him. Thinking that he'd miraculously wriggled off the hook of parental wrath, Jerry found himself on it again after a forty-eight-hour delay. Schmidt wondered at himself. His rage never seemed real to him. It certainly seemed real enough to Jerry, but not so real that the report cards ever changed. The pattern of bad grades and fatherly upset had begun when

Jerry was in fourth grade and had become so corrosive that, over the last year, Jerry had essentially stopped talking to his father about anything going on in his life. Schmidt issued edicts; Jerry shrugged his shoulders, nonchalantly agreed to everything, and then just ignored it.

Schmidt was no more successful in getting his children to pick up after themselves. Every morning, Schmidt got up at 6:00, showered, and walked to the kitchen, stepping over his son's size-twelve sneakers and thongs, his wife's sneakers, his daughter's tennis shoes and sandals, and, he had to admit, his own Clarks. The living room would be papered with discarded homework, the week's issues of the *Free Press*, glasses and mugs would be everywhere, furniture moved around, the kids' textbooks on tables and floor. Combs, brushes, wrappers from chewing gum, dirty dishes from evening snacks, dirty silverware, milk-encrusted cereal bowls, the week's mail rose from the kitchen island like Mt. Vesuvius, glued to the tile by rings of sticky spilt Kool-Aid. On the couches, half-open backpacks disgorged books and papers. Nowhere to walk without hitting a booby trap, nowhere to sit without rearranging and cleaning. Even the dog, a big white lab mix, was in on it, having raided the wastebasket for yogurt containers and taken them to her lair between the couch and the sliding-glass door. At times he felt his household was a madly spinning star, hurling chunks of itself into outer space, and he was desperately hanging on, dodging the shrapnel.

The chaos had never bothered Renee very much. "The kids are turning the whole house into their bedrooms," he'd say, desperate for an ally. She'd nod, placid amidst the waste. His children had not felt ill at ease about what they created, though their rooms were stratified with weeks of dirty clothing.

It caused them lots of trouble. Laura and Jerry lost homework, textbooks, their own CDs, other people's house keys (when they took care of vacationing neighbors' pets), library books. Various objects would enter their rooms and disappear completely. There were panicked searches for computer disks, homework directions, and school projects "due today," and parents were desperately begged for help. But this changed nothing. Threats, incentives, consequences: no result. They were almost grown-up. How would they ever cope with the world? What could he do to get them ready?

In a year, Laura would be in college, in three years, Jerry. Schmidt had made a conscious decision that once they were eighteen, he'd not offer advice, not interfere, not, in fact, parent. He would hold to this, because he'd felt smothered by advice from his parents after he was eighteen. In the meantime, he had a rush job. Don't chew with your mouth open. Elbows off the table. Apply a razor blade to that upper lip. You didn't use deodorant today, did you? He couldn't quite believe he was saying these things, and saying them again and again.

Schmidt worried about his son for specific reasons and about his daughter on general principles. Laura was smart and worked so hard in school that he wished sometimes she'd ease up, have more fun. She was sweet and considerate, and he wanted other people to see it too. He wished he could make her feel happier about herself.

Schmidt had watched his son getting more sedentary, and fatter and fatter, throughout junior high. All the kid had done was sit in front of the TV with the Nintendo on, absorbed in one game after another. The music from the games, the punching, gouging, and blood-spattering karate killer games especially, had gotten on Schmidt's nerves so much that he'd thought seriously of destroying the TV set. He had pushed Jerry to play football through junior high, to finally encounter a challenge that manifested itself off the TV screen or computer monitor, and to his relief, Jerry had stuck with the game, and even become something of a fanatic about it. At the same time, Schmidt worried that his son might get hurt, come out of football with a smashed-up knee, or a head injury, or a bad back.

Now, Jerry had lost his fat and gotten enormous. The kid was already six feet tall, and his size-twelve feet promised more inches to come. He had a butch haircut that would have passed in Marine Corps basic training. He lifted weights all year round for a fanatical football coach, and when Schmidt bumped into him, in the kitchen, in the hall, on the way to the TV set, it was like hitting a wall: Schmidt bounced, but Jerry never deviated from course. Schmidt realized that this was the year when the curve of his own declining physical vigor had intersected with that of his boy's rising strength. Now, the gap would just increase. Jerry would be able to out–bench-press him, if he couldn't already.

"I keep forgetting things," Schmidt complained to Renee one evening.

"That's because your brain cells are dying," Jerry said, looking up from the computer, where he was playing a game with plenty of gunfire and explosions.

"My brain cells are dying?"

"They start dying after you're thirty," Jerry said. Then he smiled: "My brain is still growing."

Then why did you finish ninth grade with two D's on your report card, Schmidt wanted to say, but he knew Jerry would sulk if he said it. Jerry scored above the ninetieth percentile in all of his standardized tests, in all of the areas, but he just didn't care about school. He had barely cleared the 2.0 average necessary to retain athletic eligibility, and that only because he'd gotten an A in PE and an A in chorus. It was hard for a professor of law to take.

If the kid was a rather unmotivated giant, he was a gentle one. He was the only person in the family who consistently could get near and pick up either of the neurotic cats that had annexed Schmidt's garage for their own use. The first cat, which had appeared during the time of Hale-Bopp, and was therefore called Comet, was a shorthaired black with huge green, perpetually alarmed eyes. Comet had started living in a bush in the front yard, but cat food and Jerry's strokes had drawn her into the garage, where she had skulked, fairly contented, until cat number two showed up. Number two moved in and claimed the garage as Cortez had Mexico. She looked like a purebred Persian and had beautiful blue eyes. Laura dubbed her "Yeowly," because she meowed continuously. Yeowly was as homicidal as Comet was paranoid, and soon Comet had taken up residence on the shelf over the washing machine while Yeowly grew in girth on an unrestricted diet of Meow Mix. Yeowly attempted to maul Comet at every opportunity, lurking behind boxes or the lawn mower, biding her time. Jerry had to carry Comet out of the garage in the daytime and back in at night, since she was too terrified to cross the garage on her own and, without Jerry's help, would have been perpetually "treed" over the washing machine.

Every night, Jerry lured Comet from out of a bush or off a rooftop into his arms and then shelved her, putting food and water beside her. Then he would pick up Yeowly—he was the only one she didn't claw—bring her inside for strokes, and put her back in the garage, on the floor. Yeowly had grown too fat to make the leap from the floor to the top of the washing machine, so Comet was safe, unless she tried to take a midnight litter box break, during which she'd almost certainly be jumped, and the feline shrieks of rage and terror from the garage would make Schmidt's teeth tingle.

Yeowly's favorite perch was the roof of Schmidt's car, although she was getting so fat she could barely make the climb up the windshield. One morning when the kids were getting into the car with Schmidt, so he could drop them at school, Laura said, "Did you know that you can find the center of gravity of anything by spinning it? Objects always spin around their center of gravity." She was taking physics. "I was thinking," she continued, "that if we spun Yeowly, we could find *her* center of gravity."

Jerry growled, "Very funny."

He was quite sensitive about the welfare of his cats.

At his daughter's voice lesson one summer afternoon, listening to her sing "Panus Angelicus," in a wobbly but angelic contralto, Schmidt decided on a complete overhaul, a forty-eight-year lube and tune. He'd start with music. He'd sing. He'd restore the lost harmony of his life, and it would have an effect on everyone around him. His placidity would calm people. His daughter would worry less. His son would be able to focus on school. The house would get neater. Schmidt believed this for all of ten seconds and then thought, well, singing itself is enough.

Three weeks and three lessons later, he was standing beside Eileen Foreman's baby grand, singing "do, re, mi, fa, soooo . . . so, fa, mi, re, dooooo, . . ." getting a good vibrato on the end. With each new "do" at the bottom of the scale he started up again, a half note higher. Eileen was surprised at how high he was getting. She opened her mouth wider as he went up to "so," encouraging him to unhinge his lower jaw. They ratcheted their way up the keyboard until he hit a "so" on which his voice finally cracked.

"You may be a tenor," she said, a little surprised. "You got the high A-flat that time." Last week she had said, "Maybe you're a baritone." Couldn't he be both? Why go with conventional boundaries? He imagined a voice that went from the lowest note on the keyboard to the highest: Tennessee Ernie Ford, meet Farinetti.

Eileen was a woman with strong opinions, who liked sheer purple dresses and had a house filled with sleepy, well-adjusted cats who liked to be picked up and petted. A big, black one named Bête Noire sprawled under the piano and yawned, displaying the bright pink top of her mouth. She paused there, in full luxury, and then snapped her mouth shut.

"Let's sing something," Eileen said. She got out a Christmas carol they'd been working on: "I Wonder as I Wander." "Just relax and feel it," she said. She kept trying to get him to emote. He sang, "I wonder as I wander, out under the sky, why Jesus the savior did come for to die, for poor ornery people like you and like I . . . I wonder as I wander, out under the sky."

She stopped. "You sound like you're talking. Use me as your imprimatur. No one else is watching. Just let it out."

He wanted to let it out. When he was a little kid, his parents had had two records, both from Broadway shows: *South Pacific* (Mary Martin and Ezio Pinza) and *L'il Abner*. He'd walk around the house belting out "I'm as corny as cabbage in August" (finding out years later that it was "Kansas in August") and "Jubilation T. Cornpone," assuming that somehow these two records were connected. Love and war and cabbage in the cornfields of Bali Hai. He played the records until his parents couldn't stand them. He sang the songs everywhere. He even sang them going up and down on a swing at school, until kids started to make fun of him for blasting out "I'm in love with a wonderful guy." (He liked Mary Martin's songs better than Ezio Pinza's.)

But now, where was that unabashed joy in song? He couldn't make progress emoting on "I wonder as I wander."

"You're *woondering*," Eileen would say, suggestively. "You're *waandering. . . .*"

He tried to picture himself, out there, wondering, wandering, and tried to connect the image to music and words.

"It's coming out flat," Eileen said. "You've got to *feel* it."

"I'm looking for an optometrist," he told Renee in mid-August, flipping through the yellow pages.

"Finally. While you're at it, you may as well get your hearing tested."

"Eileen says I have a good ear. Maybe *you* should look for an elocutionist."

"We've got hearing aids now that you can tuck right in your ear. Nobody can see them. Digital, programmable hearing aids."

"I don't want a microchip in my ear."

"There's nothing like beer," she said.

"What?"

She stared at him for a second.

"Beer?" he said.

"NO," she said. "There's nothing to FEAR."

"Don't you tell people not to stick things in their ears?"

"Yes. But that's different."

"Just speak more plainly, and I'll be fine. I can hear you. You just slur everything together."

"How will you get any pleasure out of torturing your law students this fall if you can't hear their responses?"

Schmidt flipped a few more pages. The ad he liked the best said, "See the world in a whole new way. Dr. Silas Blumenthal, O. D."

The next Wednesday, before his lesson with Eileen, he was in Dr. Blumenthal's chair, staring through an opthalmoscope, having a remarkably difficult time deciding whether he could see better through one lens or another, as Dr. Blumenthal flipped them back and forth. Is this better, or is this better? Is this better, or is this better?

"About the same now?" Dr. Blumenthal often asked.

"Yes."

Blumenthal concluded, "You should have come to me sooner. You need bifocals, and you've needed them for a long time."

"I'm only forty-eight."

"Some people need them sooner than others. Forty-eight's typical."

"My father was an optometrist. It's a little hard for me to go to other optometrists."

"Your father died?"

"Seventeen years ago. At fifty-nine."

"Too soon, too soon." Dr. Blumenthal shook his white head sadly. Dr. Blumenthal's hands reminded Schmidt of his grandmother's: long, delicate fingers, very wrinkled, and yet steady and strong. A week later, when the glasses arrived, Dr. Blumenthal adjusted the frames. "Bifocals take a while to get used to," he said, "but now, watch the world come into focus," and he patted Schmidt on the back.

For a week, the glasses felt like they were pulling Schmidt's eyes out of his head, and for another week, he had trouble remembering to move his eyes up and down instead of his head.

On back-to-school night, the teachers all told the parents to make sure they checked their kids' homework. Parents could find out about grades each week—all they had to do was get their kids to ask for progress reports. Schmidt realized he'd been negligent about this. He would assume, more or less, that his daughter was working hard. He could not assume that about his son. Weekly progress reports: that's what he wanted.

"Let's talk to Jerry about it," Renee said.

It was impossible for Schmidt to do these two-on-one parental conferences without feeling like a bully or like he was impersonating any of half a dozen sitcom fathers from the sixties.

Renee found Jerry and sat him on the living room sofa. He knew that this was his mother's family conference tableau. His eyes darted from one parent to another, and he squeezed a pillow in his fist

"We think you've got a really big year coming, . . ." Renee started.

"This year your grades really count for college admissions," Schmidt added.

"And we think you might be better off without so many, ah, distractions . . ."

". . . especially Nintendo," Schmidt said.

". . . and Sega," Renee finished.

"And so, we'd like you to put the video games away for a year . . . maybe. . . ."

"In fact, we insist on it," Schmidt said, eyeing his wife with a little impatience. "You could even get rid of them altogether. You're getting too old for them anyway. You can put the computer in the living room in your bedroom and use it to do homework. You can't get any more D's this year."

Renee looked at Schmidt doubtfully.

"OK?" Renee said to Jerry.

"Yeah. OK. I guess," Jerry said.

"We're not trying to punish you," Renee said.

"Since I haven't really done anything."

"We just want you to concentrate on school this year," Schmidt said.

"You don't seem very happy about it," Renee probed, worried, apologetic.

Good grief, Schmidt thought.

"It's OK," Jerry said. "I guess I'll just sell it all."

"You don't have to do that!" Renee said in alarm.

"I guess I will," Jerry said sadly. "No sense having the stuff if I can't play it."

"We'd like you to get weekly progress reports too," Schmidt said.

"You can get them from your teachers every Friday," Renee said.

"I know all about progress reports," Jerry mumbled.

Jerry sold the Nintendo and Sega machines and all the games. Schmidt got a new iMac, put it in the living room, and passed down his perfectly good Power Mac to Jerry, so he could do homework in his room, on the computer, uninterrupted, with the stipulation that computer games were not to be played Sunday through Thursday. "We'll trust him not to play computer games," Schmidt told his wife. "We can't police everything."

"That's a mistake," Renee said.

"The computer has replaced the typewriter. He needs one."

For the next week after football, Jerry went to his room as soon as he got home and stayed there, except for a brief dinner appearance. He was studying, he said. He remembered progress reports every other week or so. His teachers made the usual comments.

"He's really angry," Renee said.

"Yup. Totally pissed."

A few weeks later, Renee walked into Jerry's room, walked back to the kitchen, and told Schmidt, "He was playing a computer game. *Civilization.*"

"Did you tell him to quit?"

"Yes."

"He knows he isn't supposed to do that."

"He said he didn't know."

"Bull," Schmidt sighed. "He's just replacing video games with computer games."

Schmidt stalked into his son's bedroom, grinding his teeth. Jerry was at the computer, typing.

"Jerry?"

"Uh, yeah, what?"

"We made it clear that there was no computer game playing during the week."

"I thought it was OK."

"No. It is not OK. Don't do it anymore."

"Not even fifteen minutes, for a homework break? That's all I was doing."

"Fifteen minutes turns into hours."

Jerry set his jaw. He wasn't going to beg.

The next week, Jerry asked for a lock on his door. "Laura's got one," he said.

"I'll get you one," Renee said. Jerry turned on his heel and went back to his bedroom.

Schmidt just shook his head.

"Laura's got one," Renee said.

"I know. I know."

Schmidt suspected computer game orgies would be going on behind that locked door while biology, geometry, and French went begging for time. And he'd never know. Those weren't rooms. They were bunkers, jungle islands in unexplored waters, the inhabitants lost to communication. On the other hand, while Jerry was at school, he could mount an expedition, wade through the junk, and check the computer.

On Tuesday morning, when he didn't have to teach, he took the kids to school, then returned home. Renee was at work. He went straight to Jerry's door and opened it.

He felt bad about this.

On the one hand, how could snooping in his son's room inspire a trusting relationship between them? On the other, he could imagine the fathers of the boys who shot up Columbine High thinking the same thing while their sons stored plastique and Uzis under their beds. So he opened the door, kicked his way through piles of clothing, Magic Cards, and tiny soldiers and trolls from some kind of game, moved a football off the desk chair, and sat down. He looked around.

In so many ways it was still a child's room. There was even the old teddy bear, sitting on the dresser. Plastic dinosaurs still spilled out of a basket in the closet. Schmidt imagined Jerry hoarding all of the pieces of his past and present, trying to put them together, as if they were part of the vast jigsaw puzzle that would become his life. At such moments, he wanted to take his son in his arms— the seven-year-old Jerry—and protect him from everything.

He turned on the computer, opened the *Civilization* file, and immediately saw games and dates for the last week. Games for every night. Boadicea of the Celts: Wednesday, 7:36 P.M. Julius Caesar of the Romans, Tuesday, 8:37 P.M. Frederick of the Germans: Monday, 7:52 P.M., etc. All this while the kid was getting a D- in chemistry and a D in algebra II. All this, after he'd told Jerry a week before to stop.

Schmidt pulled power cables out of the wall, and placed the monitor, printer, and cables on the computer. Then he picked up all of it on his forearms, put his chin on top of the monitor to steady it, and headed for the basement, jaw clenched. The dog, Tashy, tagged after him, bouncing against his legs, tongue lolling sycophantically. He had reached the door to the garage, the basement stairs going down to his left, when he heard a nerve-severing shriek. Without thinking, he got a hand free, and opened the door. The black cat, Comet, normally terrified of entering the house, backed into his ankles trying to escape the bared fangs and flashing claws of Yeowly, who apparently had decided to finish off her rival, once and for all. In a fit of blood rage, one cat bore down on the other, and Tashy, utterly astonished, stood transfixed as a ball of black fur careened down the stairwell, pursued by a gray hairball, both of which emitted the operatic sounds of a feline Göttesdämmerung.

Tashy bolted between Schmidt's legs like a linebacker going after a fumble. She ran and skidded down the stairs, legs going in all directions, as Schmidt fought to keep from going over headfirst. Through a desperate application of will, and a forced rearrangement of his skeletal system, Schmidt and everything he carried hung together, as he righted himself on the creaking stairway.

He peered over the monitor at the wooden stairs, lowering his eyes, so that, for a moment, he was staring through the bottom part of his bifocals and seeing the stairs in a blur. The sounds of tooth and claw echoed in conjunction throughout the basement. Part of the blur before Schmidt contained an elongated image which he could not identify, and which he was not paying any particular attention to, given the chaos from below.

Schmidt put his foot on the image, which in fact was a book bag that Jerry had quickly removed from the living room the night before, when Schmidt had complained there was nowhere to sit. It contained Jerry's homework and books, which he had forgotten to take to school, and which, at that very moment, at the beginning of Mrs. Ritter's algebra II class, Jerry was wishing he had with him.

Schmidt put his foot on the book bag, which slid, and he twisted, like a top, spun off a table. "Aaaiiieee!" he screamed, and down he went, monitor in front, feet rising behind in an attempted Immelman that was quickly arrested by the stairs. The monitor smashed, the printer disintegrated on the basement floor, and Schmidt cartwheeled down the steps, his head finally bouncing against the cement at the bottom, as the rest of his body crashed around him.

The first thing that intruded itself on Schmidt's aching consciousness was his leg. He was a boom box with the volume turned to a deafening level, and the tune he played was pain. From his right shin, the sensation came red and blinding. After registering this for a while, he noticed a companion pain in his right shoulder, which on its own would have demanded a great deal of attention, but given the competition, it came in a distant second.

Bits of smashed glass from the monitor were all over the floor. A few shards were sticking into Schmidt's hand, but his overloaded circuits registered no pain from this. He pulled out the glass. Blood flowed liberally. He tried to right himself and sit up. The impossible happened. The pain got worse. So much worse that Schmidt thought a portal to another world had opened, a world from which bright, pain-filled light rushed as if into a vacuum. Schmidt felt faint and lay back. He lay there until his faculties returned, until the thinking part of his brain developed some kind of truce with the part that registered pain, so that both could work at the same time. He heard animal sounds from upstairs, the battle having shifted ground. Had the animals just run over him? Had Yeowly murdered Comet before Tashy had gotten the both of them? He delicately felt his shin, and the lump there screamed when he touched it. He wondered if he had a compound fracture. He felt his right shoulder. Broken collarbone? Did he have a concussion? A lump was rising under his left eyebrow. Renee wouldn't be home for hours.

The stairs were steep, and he doubted that he could sit up, let alone get to the top.

He waited. A half hour? Five minutes? No sounds came from upstairs. Not even a woof. If he could turn himself around, maybe he could inch up, putting his butt on first one step, then the next, then the next, and finally get to the top. It would hurt like crazy. It might take hours. But, he decided, it would be better than lying on the concrete just waiting.

Using his left elbow and leg, he swiveled himself around so that his head was pointed at the staircase. Each movement elicited a soaring flash of protest from shin and collarbone. Then he pushed off with his left foot and elbow, getting his head onto the first stair, then his shoulders, then the small of his back, then his buttocks, and so on up the stairs. He'd been doing a lot of screaming. He decided he'd try to sing instead.

Stay focused, he thought. Try to make notes. On each step he sang, "Do, re, mi, fa, soooo . . . so, fa, mi, re, dooooo," going a half-step up the chromatic scale each time he went up a whole stair step. He paused whenever he felt a moment of vertigo so overpowering that he thought he'd lose consciousness, but he did not want to stop for long. "Do, re, mi, fa, so, laaaaaaagh!" his fractured bones sang.

When he got to the top of the stairs, and his voice broke, he was certain he'd gotten higher than A-flat. He used the same technique to push himself across the floor to the phone on the living room desk. He didn't know how to reach the phone, so he found the cord and pulled it to the floor. The receiver bounded around and Schmidt heard the beautiful dial tone. He called 9-1-1, and when the medics arrived at the locked house, they broke through the living room's sliding-glass door to get in. In addition to Schmidt, they found one cat under a bed in Jerry's room, one on top of the dresser in Laura's room, and a frustrated dog running back and forth, trying to squeeze under the bed to get Yeowly or leap high enough to get Comet. They took Schmidt to Community Hospital, only a few floors up from where Renee worked.

He spent the next twenty-four hours in the hospital while the doctors observed him to rule out any serious head injury. His leg was in a cast and his arm in a sling. Immobilization irritated him more than pain. He thought about how he could use his current condition to humorous effect when he taught torts.

"Don't yell at Jerry," Renee told him. "He feels just terrible about this. Yesterday he cried. He's still a little kid in so many ways. Both of the kids went on a cleaning spree. You should see their rooms."

"Did you talk to him about the computer games?"

"Yes."

"And?"

"He feels miserable about that too."

"Well, I guess I took care of the computer problem."

"The paramedics don't know how you made it up the stairs. You're a raven," she said, and kissed him on the forehead.

He didn't ask for clarification.

He staggered around home on one crutch, arm still in a sling. "Does it hurt, Dad?" Jerry asked him for the dozenth time.

"No."

"I'm sorry."

"For what?"

"Everything. The backpack. Playing the computer." Jerry looked like he was going to burst into tears. Schmidt could not stand the thought of his 230-pound son crying.

"I love you. I want you to know that. If you want to play with the computer a little at night, out in the living room, go ahead. Take a break once in a while. I just want you to be ready for the world. Nobody ever is. Nobody ever is ready." Even as he was saying all this, as much as he wanted Jerry to believe it, the words left a stale aftertaste. Did his son feel the same way? He looked into his eyes and couldn't tell.

"In a couple years, there won't be much I can do for you any-more. You won't want me to tell you what to do, and I won't be able to anyway. Maybe I can't even now. But you need to get ready." Schmidt couldn't come up with anything better. He had too many models, his own father, too many TV fathers, all offer-ing their scripts, and none were good enough. Maybe the lie was that being a good father meant coming up with the right piece of dialogue. When he shut up, his son looked back at him from the great distance of relief.

"Sure," he said, and shrugged.

To Schmidt's surprise, tears started to form in his eyes. "Is it something I've done? Are you mad at me? Is that why you're not trying in school? Are you mad at me because I'm on your back too much?"

Jerry looked at him, as if something had caught in his throat.

"Because if you're mad at me, if I've been a jerk, I'm sorry. Don't mess up your life because you're mad at me. I'm not perfect. But I love you."

"Dad . . . Dad . . . it's OK." Jerry said, patting his crying father on the back. "Don't hurt yourself to get back at me," Schmidt said.

In a few weeks, the kids' bedrooms were back to their usual mess, the mess was spilling over into the rest of the house, and

Schmidt began to feel better. Underneath his cast, his leg itched like crazy. At night in bed, his collarbone plagued him. He doubted that Jerry would make any miraculous improvements in school. But maybe he would. Someday, he might put his intelligence to work. Whatever, Schmidt felt like he'd dumped a load of crap from his system.

The next week he hobbled to his voice lesson on crutches. After Eileen took him through the usual warm-ups, she set some music on the piano. Schmidt edged in behind her. It was a song he hadn't heard since grade school. She played, and he sang:

Sleep my child and peace attend thee
All through the night.
Guardian angels God will send thee
All through the night.

As he sang, he thought of tucking his children in bed and his daughter's fears when she was young, how her vast imagination filled the dark with monsters. He'd read her stories, sung her songs, made up stories, and every time he'd tried to leave, she'd grabbed at him, her fear overcoming her tiredness. Finally, he'd have to leave, knowing she was terrified, despite night-lights, despite knowing her parents were just in the other room. He remembered his son, apparently with none of his daughter's fears, so trusting, clutching a stuffed bear in one arm and a stuffed dog in another, eyes so clear, confident that he was protected.

"Beautiful," Eileen said. "What were you thinking of?"

GASERS

It is evening in Fresno, the butt end of a 105-degree day that's still burning. The air has a chemical tang, and ozone rises over the city in an invisible plume. August has been tinder dry, and tankers have been flying over the city for weeks, dousing fires in the Sierra Nevada. Tonight, though, mugginess lies over the city like a steamy blanket. Most people in Fresno stay inside when it gets this way, like midwesterners hunkering down during a blizzard. They stay inside to avoid the chemically brewed air. They set their thermostats to seventy-five or eighty, and let the air conditioners blast away, despite jacked-up power bills. Ceiling fans whirl, and the power grid strains from Seattle to San Diego. Suzanne Gilmore, who is in a movie theater with her daughter, enduring *Planet of the Apes,* is just happy to be in a cool, dark spot. Gorillas beat on each other and toss Mark Wahlberg great distances. He bounces well. She thinks of her son at football practice and hopes he has as much bounce.

A few miles away Tom Gilmore is sitting down in rickety high school bleachers, amidst a gaggle of parents, to watch the end of football practice. He sits next to Randall Frey, a man he has gotten to know slightly, over the years, because of their sons' friendship. Matt Gilmore and Colin Frey have been inseparable since fifth grade, when the Freys moved to Fresno from Poulsbo, Washington. Frey manages a Winston tire shop, where Tom got his last set of tires, even though Costco has better prices.

"Who's winning?"

"They're really working 'em over pretty good," Randall responds, "they" being the coaches.

"Hope they've been giving them a lot of water." No one in the little group that shows up to watch practice ever says "heatstroke," but this fall, the phrase hangs in the collective mind because of the training-camp death, just a few weeks before, of Viking tackle Korey Stringer.

The team is, in fact, taking a water break, milling around a big cart that has half a dozen green watercoolers, getting drinks, wadding up paper cups, spraying themselves with water bottles. Tom tries to see his son, Matt, jersey sixty-five, but can't find him. He sees Colin, though, a big, strong-looking kid who is benchpressing his weight of 260 pounds. Colin plays offensive tackle, and the coach is counting on him to take big hunks out of defensive lines.

"When I played they didn't let us have water during a practice," Tom says, shaking his head. "Then, they didn't believe in it. Thought it would cramp you up."

"Yeah," Randall says, "I remember that. Bear Bryant started that. At half-time we got a slice or two of orange. That was it."

The sun has bled out against the western horizon, and the first stars are out. In the lights over the field, thousands of incandescent moths, drunk on light, beat their powdery wings, seeking to bubble themselves against hot glass. Tom's shirt sticks to him, squishes under his arms. He wishes he had a bottle of water, but he's happy. A football field is a fascinating place when the nightlights are on, a place utterly artificial and yet more real than it would be in daylight. He remembers lighted fields as places of strange clarity.

This is the first day of full pads, and the kids have soaked their jerseys and pants, as if they've sweated through plastic, pads, everything. When the water break is over, the backs and ends jog off to the far end of the field, and the interior linemen go into a drill. In groups of three, two offensive lineman, one defensive, they practice down blocks. Tom spots Matt, a squat figure who looks like he might go rolling across the field if someone collided with him. "Come across hard," the line coach, Nat Hernandez, keeps yelling at the defensive players. "You only hurt us when you lay back." But the defensive linemen aren't coming across hard, and the blockers aren't hitting hard. When they do hit, they don't keep their feet churning when they make contact, which they must do to push people off the line of scrimmage and make holes. Matt, otherwise known as "Toad," a family nickname that has, since elementary school, been public property, hits his man and leans on him, like a punch-drunk prizefighter, pushing up with his legs but not churning his feet. "Damn it Toad," Hernandez says, "keep your feet *pumpin'*. When you don't give everything you've got, you cheat this team." As second-string center, Toad may be lucky to play fifteen minutes of football the entire season, but Hernandez chews him out as if he were a starter. *That's respect,* Toad explains. *There are people on the team so miserable and inept that the coaches don't even get down on them anymore.*

The small bunch of parents in the bleachers watches the practice morosely. Two mothers are complaining about how long it's taking. "They were supposed to be done at 7:30. When are they supposed to do their homework?" one asks. "They're all just going to go home and drop."

"When Kyle gets home, he can't even eat."

"And then they're supposed to get up tomorrow morning at 6:30," the other one groans. "They can't even *walk* at 6:30."

"They've been here since 3:00."

"I don't like the language these coaches use," one says, but in fact, it's hard to hear what the coaches are saying. Once in a while, a word or two comes through.

"State law says practices can't go over two and a half hours," a father grins and shrugs. "That makes it . . . nearly six hours now."

"Closer to eight if you take into account weights in the morning," Randall Frey says.

"And they're always late. You never know when they're going to get done. They say 7:30, and here it is, an hour later. I think somebody needs to talk to those coaches."

"That's because the coach is Armenian," Andy Garabedian, another bleacher regular says. "There's *odar* time—that's the regular time all you *odars* keep—and then there's Armenian time, which runs an hour or two later."

Tom doesn't know about *odar* time, but the rest is all true. As usual, Tom had dropped Toad off at the gym for weight lifting and conditioning at 6:15 in the morning and watched the team sleepwalk across the north gym parking lot like *Night of the Living Dead*.

"When I played high school football, we practiced two hours a night, tops," Tom says to Randall. "We were home by 6:00. Parents would have rebelled at this." The mystery, he thinks, is why *we* don't. *How*, he wonders, *did high school football go from what he knew as a kid to a forty-hour-a-week job?*

"Colin has a hell of a cold," his father says. "Down in his chest." It was a piece of data that a parent will just toss into the air, a little petition. Then, as if to erase this little bit of negativism, he adds, "I never would have made it through basic training if it hadn't been for high school football."

Tom looks at Randall's potbelly and at Andy Garabedian's, which is just huge. Then he considers his own. *How*, he wonders, *did we ever play football? How did we ever get like this?*

After more drills, the team runs plays for another half hour. The end of practice approaches, which the team yearns for but dreads. First, they'll do an unknown number of "Green Bays." (It is the indeterminacy of the number that is really frightening.) Then, to finish practice, they'll do "gasers," also of an indeterminate number, running back and forth the width of the football field. Backs and ends will have to get back and forth twice in under forty seconds; linemen in under fifty. Toad hates gasers worse than just about anyone because he almost never makes it under fifty, and the line gets down on him, because if anyone doesn't make it under fifty, it's *more* gasers.

"But that's only in theory," Toad sometimes tells Colin, when they try to fathom what goes on in the minds of their coaches.

"They never tell us how many we'd have to do at the beginning, so how do we know we're getting extra? They really just give us as many as they want. Coaches are Impressionists," Toad the art historian explains. "They apply gasers as the mood strikes them." Colin also dreads gasers and actually has more trouble with them than Toad. Toad doesn't let results get to him. Securely sunk into the second string, he has a more philosophical approach to looking bad than Colin. Toad's body wobbles from side to side when he runs, and he has concluded it would violate the laws of aerodynamics for him to do a gaser in under fifty. It would also probably violate thermodynamic principles, which claim that a system cannot expend more energy than has been put into it. "I am thermodynamically disadvantaged," Toad explains.

Instead of going straight to Green Bays and gasers, however, Coach Arkanian calls the team to the middle of the field, where they all take a knee. Toad is next to Colin, who haraughs up a clod of gunk from his lungs and spits it out on the ground. For a few moments, hope surges though the team that *this* is the end of practice, that since they've worked so hard already, and since it's the first day of pads, that Green Bays and gasers are off. A final pep talk, and the coach will dismiss them for the night. This is what they hope, but none of them believes it.

Coach Arkanian, surrounded by forty football players and nearly a dozen coaches, puts his hands on his hips and gazes around him in disgust.

"Practice tonight stunk. You're not putting your hearts into it. The blocking drills stink. The tackling stinks. You receivers—I don't know how you can seem to be running and stay in the same place so long. The idea of running is to traverse distance over time. The idea of running a deep route is to outdistance the defender, not waltz with him. You guys just don't want to play football. You stand around in a stupor, scared of pain. You stand around feeling sorry for yourselves. What a bunch of whiners." Coach Arkanian scans the team again. He looks as if he's had to swallow a small turd.

He lowers his voice: "You may think we're driving you too

hard. Mothers call and complain to me. Practices are too long. Their babies are too tired when they get home. I don't want you telling your mothers how hard practice is. If they ask you about practice, just say, 'Practice was wonderful.' You complain to your mothers, and your mothers complain to me, and I don't want to hear from them. What do *they* know?

"Before I came to this high school you had teams that went 6-5 or 5-6. You had easy coaches, and you lost a lot of games. Well, last year we went 9-3 and this year we can do better. I want to win, and to win, you have to pay the price. I know you're sacrificing. But the coaches sacrifice too. You may think your practices are too long, but they're long for the coaches too, and we spend hours besides, looking at game films, scouting other teams, planning practices. If you don't want to pay the price, then quit right now. Some of you guys think you can win if you don't pay the price. Or maybe you don't care about winning that much. If you feel that way, you should get off the team now. Quit. Be a quitter. But if you're going to stay on the team, you've got to be willing to sacrifice. OK? You've been holding back, like a bunch of cowards. Now we're going to be the best fourth-quarter team in the valley, win or lose. The best in the fourth quarter. That's when you show character. Guts. Testicular fortitude. So let's get at it."

Colin and Toad look at each other: *Testicular fortitude?*

It's just not on, old bean, thinks Toad the Monty Python fan.

"Finally," one of the mothers says, when they see the team huddle at the middle of the field.

"Do you think they're going to let them go?"

"I don't know. Can you hear what he's saying?"

"Maybe they're done for the night."

"Fat chance," chuckles Andy Garabedian.

"Wonder what they're talking about," somebody says.

"My coach used to tell us that if we drank beer, rode Hondas, and chased girls all the time, all we'd turn into is a bunch of beer drinkin,' Honda ridin' girl chasers."

"Bet you didn't want to turn into that."

The players break out of the team huddle, sprint to the sideline and spread out. Andy Garabedian takes out a handkerchief and mops his square jowls. Tom readjusts his spine. Randall Frey feels suddenly that he needs to take several deep breaths, that the air just doesn't have enough oxygen.

By the time they've done thirty or forty Green Bays, Toad can't keep up with the whistle. It's OK, he thinks, because Colin can't either. When the whistle blows he's supposed to go down, hit the ground, then get back up and run in place until the whistle blows again, when he's supposed to go down into a push-up position, boom, flat on his chest, and then get up and jog in place some more, but the whistle just isn't giving him time enough to get up, so he often gets just halfway up, to his knees, maybe, before the whistle blows again and then boom, down he goes, tries to get up, whistle, boom, tries to get up, whistle, boom . . . but he sees Colin having even more trouble, and he figures he's doing OK, only backs can even come close to doing this drill, those little thin bastards, whistle, boom, up, this time he gets all the way up, damn! whistle, down. Ends can do it too, this up/down crap. Colin sounds like he's breathing through wet cotton, and sometimes he has to skip a few up/downs to hack something up and spit it out. Colin doesn't have time to both breathe and cough while doing up/downs. The world begins to spin around. *No one expects the Spanish Inquisition,* Toad thinks. And then it's time for gasers. *How many Green Bays altogether?* Toad wonders. *Felt like a new record. Gasers. After gasers: done. Make it through gasers, you get water, you get to go home, where I'll drink a couple gallons of water. Then chemistry. AP chemistry till midnight.* He doesn't think he'll be able to hold down anything solid until breakfast, but he won't be awake enough to eat breakfast.

Backs and ends always go first at gaser time. "All the way to the other side and touch down on the sideline," Coach Hernandez yells. The backs and ends go off, and as they come back Hernandez counts the seconds: "fifteen, sixteen, seventeen. . . ." They touch down. Back across the field they go, touch down on the sideline, and come tearing back. Everybody makes it in under forty.

Fifty seconds for the linemen. *Pace yourself,* Toad thinks. Do this in exactly fifty seconds. He smacks Colin on the back, and Colin can only nod, cough, and spit. But when Hernandez says, "OK linemen. Go!" Toad thinks, *Shit, if I had sixty seconds, I'd never make it. Coaches are insane. I've given myself over to maniacs.* But off he goes, at a pace that emphasizes self-preservation. *We're going to do a lot of these,* Toad guesses. *Best to hold a little something in reserve.*

Toad's legs lope along with a mind of their own, and he sees a bunch of people, all taller than he is, thumping toward the sideline. Colin pounds along beside him, sucking great hunks out of Mother Earth's atmosphere, a space-monster threatening the planet with asphyxiation. Toad has never heard a sound like it before. "C'mon Colin," Toad gasps, "We gotta get back in fifty. . . ."

When linemen reach the sideline, they're supposed to touch down with one hand but only a couple of them do it, those damn guards who always wanted to be halfbacks anyway. Tonight, the coaches aren't yelling at them for not touching down. If they really wanted to get down on the team, they'd watch close, one at each end of the field. Toad figures this into his calculations. *These gasers will be horrendous,* he guesses, *but not the ultimately horrendous puking-your-guts-out gasers.* At the second turn, Toad and Colin are in dead last, along with Mike Lassiter, a kid who is even less likely to see playing time than Toad. Colin is barely getting his feet off the ground. He's scuffing his cleats in the grass. Toad would like to give him more encouragement, but he can't waste air.

When they make their second about-face, and he is heading once again to the far sideline, Toad knows they will never make it back in under fifty. He thinks he's already heard Hernandez shout out twenty-nine. He doesn't see Colin. He doesn't see Lassiter. He doesn't see anything in its particularity. He only sees the sideline. He doesn't know how many seconds it takes him to finish. He doesn't know when Colin or Lassiter make the finish. He just knows that they're going to do more gasers, an infinite number of gasers, or at least as many as Coach Arkanian wants, because he will never make this trip in under fifty seconds. Hell, he'll never make it in under sixty. He and Colin and Lassiter straggle in and get a break while the backs do their second gaser. *Take your time*, Toad thinks.

Each gaser is worse, if that's possible. The copper taste foams up from Toad's lungs as if they are dissolving. His head pounds. His legs feel leaden. The team yells at him and Colin and Lassiter because they aren't making it, but he doesn't care. When he runs, the world is no bigger than the space he occupies. He is in his own tight little world of pain. There could be an earthquake; the field could be bombarded with debris from a meteorite shower. He'd just keep plunging straight ahead.

They do four, five, six—eight more gasers.

At the sideline, when the backs and ends take their turn, the interior linemen hold their arms up, hands locked behind their helmets. It makes breathing easier. Hernandez yells, "OK. One more. Make it a good one. *If anyone dogs it, you're goin' again.*"

Colin doesn't look good. His face is red as a stoplight. His eyes bulge, and his chest heaves. "One more," Toad gasps. "Just one more and we're outta here."

Colin just looks at him. Can't talk, but bobs his head. Toad bangs his fist on Colin's shoulder pad.

By gaser number four, the parents can tell the team is past tired. The mothers feel their children are being tortured. The coach is a sadist. He hates kids. They are sure he wants to kill the team *before* they have any games. The line coach counts down the seconds: "forty-eight, forty-nine, fifty."

At about five feet, six inches and 210 pounds, Toad reminds his father of Frosty the Snowman trying to do sprints, a round head atop a round body. Toad is starting to hobble a little. He is still recovering from a February arthroscopy for a torn meniscus. A torn meniscus and he never even started, never even got hit, Tom thinks. He just ground up the cartilage gradually. But now he's back doing squats with three hundred pounds. "I'm rehabbed," Toad claims.

The team does more gasers, and as Toad and Colin fall farther behind, the team starts to get down on them. Some of the kids are encouraging—"Come on, Toad, gut it out"—but others get just plain ugly. "Get your friggin' butt in gear, Gilmore." "Come on, lard ass, we don't wanna be here all night." Colin Frey takes less abuse. He's a starter. But he's coming in behind Toad.

"Jeez," Randall Frey says, thinking of his son's lungs. Cold. Bronchitis maybe.

Tom is grinding his teeth. It is excruciating to hear the whole line jeer at your son.

When the team finishes the gaser, Lassiter lies on his back and gasps.

"Get up Lassiter!" Hernandez roars. "It's the fourth quarter, we're on the twenty-yard line, and we've just got a few minutes left to score. Are you gonna give up? Are you gonna give up?" Hernandez screams. Toad imagines a crack opening in Hernandez's forehead and little scorpions pouring out, running all over his face. "C'mon Lassiter. Get off the ground! I don't want to see *anybody* on the ground during gasers, ever again, unless you're dying. I don't want to see you on the ground *unless you are dead!*"

"Quit bending over. Stand tall! You want the other team to see you all bent over in the huddle? Everybody, stand tall! If you haven't got the guts for this, you haven't got the guts to play Friday, or maybe even the Friday after that. . . ." Hernandez is getting worked up now. "Lassiter, I don't want to see you on the ground unless you've had a fatal heart attack. I want you to be dead before you hit the ground. Then we'll know *for sure* you can't play."

The next set of gasers, Lassiter is on the ground again. Hernandez gapes at Lassiter as if he were some unknown life-form that just dropped onto the field from above. Then he takes his clipboard, holds it at arm's length, and smacks it into his forehead. The report echoes across the field.

When Suzanne Gilmore and her daughter get home from *Planet of the Apes,* she starts making supper—cold salad with elbow noodles. It's past 8:00, but she's learned over the last couple of years that Tom and Toad probably won't be home before 9:00. At first, Toad won't want to eat, but eventually, after he's had the chance to calm down, he will. She makes hamburger patties, puts charcoal in the kettle grill, which she decides to light around quarter to nine, whether they're back or not. Every fall she tries to convince her husband that their only son shouldn't play football. The parameters of the conversation are always the same.

"He's exhausted all the time. He doesn't have enough time to keep up with his schoolwork," she says.

"He does get pretty good grades, though."

"Not as good as he could get. And he's never going to play much anyway. I don't understand why he even wants to do it."

"He loves being part of the team. It gives him an identity. And confidence. At least that's what it gave me. And a kid his age needs that. It's part of growing up."

"Is it worth wrecking his knee for? Maybe he'll want to use his legs someday."

"Look," Tom always says, "do you want me to tell him he can't play? What will that do to him? Right now it's his *life.*"

"That's the problem! It shouldn't be. Football corrupts people. It's for parents, now, not the kids, a bunch of superachiever parents who wield their children like weapons. They want a coach who'll do the job for them, win for them, and they kept firing coaches until they got Arkanian, who is obliged to be just as corrupt and crazy as they are. How can men be so dense? So helpless? You're all helpless in front of the big football machine." But Tom always looks at her as if she were some kind of alien, incapable of understanding the momentous secret value of self-destruction.

She squirts twice as much lighter fluid into the kettle grill as she needs, scratches a match and flips it in.

⊷ ⊱◈⊰ ⊶

The linemen gasp on the sideline. Hernandez paces back and forth, wearing a rut in the grass. He stops in front of Toad and grabs his facemask. "Be a man, Toad!" Hernandez bellows. "You want to be a Toad all your life? You want to grow up to be a Toad? A little hippity, hoppity fat-ass Toad? Frey, you've been loafing all night. Jeez, you guys disgust me. Conserving your energy. Afraid to hurt."

Toad is not an angry person. Mild dislike qualified by self-doubt is usually the most violent emotion he can summon up. But the unreasonableness of Hernandez's insults, the injustice of them, after over seven hours of practice, takes Toad to a level of rage he has never experienced. It brings tears to his eyes. Colin is hacking away, hands on hips, like he's just inhaled a glass of water. The rest of the line is glaring at them both, everyone with their hands on theirs hips or behind their helmets, trying to get as much air as possible. The backs have almost finished their gaser, and Hernandez checks his stopwatch. "Good job, *backs and ends*," he yells, looking at the line. "Backs and ends are done. Hit the showers. You probably won't see the line until tomorrow morning, so say good-night to them. The line doesn't care whether it gets home tonight. The line may be here until midnight. They may still be running when you get to school tomorrow. They may die. But it won't matter, because they haven't learned to block anyway."

Toad would like to break Hernandez in two. He'd like to feed him his clipboard piece by busted piece. He'd like to file down the man's whistle until it's razor sharp and open up an incision in him from chin to navel, scoop out his guts, and stomp on his entrails.

"OK, linemen," Hernandez yells, "give me a good one!"

Toad tears down the field in a fantasy of revenge. He has been resurrected by hatred. He feels a surge of energy and decides he's not going to come in third to last. He will kill to be first, and if he doesn't finish first, he will kill Hernandez. He, Toad, will kill himself, if that's what it takes, and so he goes into a suicide sprint. And when he gets to the point where he has nothing left, when his legs and lungs are ready to cut out altogether, a miracle happens.

The Second Wind comes upon Toad, the athlete's Pentecost.

He feels a surge of joy, and energy, from out of nowhere, joy mixed with the seething desire to tear off Hernandez's head. He's pumping. He's passing people. Nobody notices, and he pumps harder. He sees himself on top of Hernandez, beating and beating him, ribs and chest giving way with great crunching sounds while he, the Great Toad, makes great Toad cries to the blood-red moon. And Hernandez is under him begging, "Please forgive me, Toad, please forgive me," and Toad has no forgiveness, no remorse. Toad hears the elation of a huge crowd, and they're all screaming, "Kill, Toad, Kill!" and now, instead of eviscerating or decapitating Hernandez, he's heading toward the goal line, he's got the ball, he's the goddamn ball carrier, he's passing all these fat guys, he's Super-Toad, and then Toad even passes himself.

When he gets back to the starting sideline he *does* hear Hernandez yell, the real Hernandez: "Ataway Toad! Twenty-two seconds! Run it out!" Toad pivots and heads across the field again. Toad believes he's going to finish in under fifty. He has decided to pass the whole line.

Tom Gilmore can't believe it. Toad is in the middle of the pack and moving up, fueled by God knows what, and Tom wants to jump up and bellow, like some dark-age Saxon tribesman, because he is seeing the very transformation of his son.

When Toad finishes—at about forty-six seconds—he's passed almost everyone. His chest is heaving; he's wobbling around. Hernandez runs over to him, and Tom can hear him shout: "See what you can do? You're an *animal*, Toad. You're a *man*," and Tom watches as Hernandez pounds his fists on Toad's shoulder pads and gives him a crunching hug.

Tom is so caught up in his son that he doesn't notice when Colin Frey drops like a marionette whose strings have been cut. But he hears a woman beside him gasp and feels Randall Frey stand up.

He sees Colin in a heap in the middle of the field. No one seems to notice at first. Then Hernandez looks back and yells, "Frey, get your butt off the ground," but Colin doesn't move. Toad hasn't spotted him yet.

Hernandez walks over. "Jeez . . . ," he says. He gets down on one knee by Frey, whose chest is heaving. "Bill," Hernandez yells to the trainer, and motions. Trainer Bill jogs over, kneels down, then sprints back to his golf cart. Arkanian is talking to some of his backfield coaches. The line is getting its breath. Toad spies Colin and jogs out too. Trainer Bill roars back across the field in his oversized golf cart. Coaches begin to gather around, and when Arkanian sees the crowd, he runs over. Coaches run to Colin, players are warned back by other coaches, and soon Colin becomes invisible within the huddle of bodies. Randall Frey is running across the field toward his son. The adults in the stands, wanting to take their kids home, stretch to see something, and decide they should stay out of the way. The team waits in confusion, some players standing where they've finished the gasers.

Tom sees Trainer Bill and one of the coaches upend a watercooler, and a cascade of ice and water pours out into the middle of the crowd. Then they grab another one and do it again. A loud shriek, as if from a mouse being devoured by a hawk, goes up from where the ice water is splashing down.

Later, Colin says he thought they were trying to drown him. "I couldn't get any air, and they were trying to drown me. Then I screamed. Gosh it was cold!"

The doctors tell Colin he's had "something like" an asthma attack, or "something like" heat exhaustion. "They just ran him out of air," is what Randall Frey says. "Trainer Bill thought he had heatstroke. But they just ran him until he couldn't breathe anymore."

Tom and Toad have followed the ambulance to St. Agnes, and they stay there until they find out that Colin is OK, not getting home until midnight. Tom calls Suzanne from the hospital at 9:30. She gets Toad home for a shower at 10:00 but brings him back to the hospital with his AP chemistry book at 11:00.

When they all finally get to bed, Suzanne tells Tom, "I want Matt out of football tomorrow. I want him out now. I want you to call that coach and tell him, *Matt is out now.* They could have killed that boy out there. He could have gotten heatstroke for all they knew, just like that guy on the Vikings. They could have killed him."

"I was scared when I saw Colin go down," Tom says. And it is true. He's been scared a few times in his life. In fights as a kid. Rock climbing. Jump school. And now he's scared for his son, and it's worse.

Tom feels the hot aura of Suzanne's body next to him. They both lie on top of the covers, and she's awake, waiting for him to put some kind of satisfactory period to this episode, to admit that she's right. The air conditioner chugs. The ceiling fan whirs. *You should have seen Toad out there tonight,* he wants to say. *You should have seen Toad run.*

THE ANGEL AT THE TOP
OF THE STAIRS

When I was seven or eight, my family lived in a house by a drive-in theater, outside a small Michigan town on Lake Huron called Harbor Beach. The house was small, with two downstairs bedrooms, my parents' and my sister's. Sometime after Nora came, I had been moved upstairs. My bedroom was at the end of a long hall flanked by two attics. The top of the stairs was at one end of the hall, my bedroom at the other. Once I saw an angel at the top of those stairs. I believe it was the only angel I will ever see, this side of the grave, though sometimes I wonder if I didn't see another one with ratty blond hair and impossibly blue eyes. I don't expect such visions to appear at my stage of life anymore, though perhaps they will at the end, when the solid world dissolves like the image of melting film on a movie screen.

Are all children an incoherent mixture of credulity and fear? I was, and I think my own children were. My family was Lutheran, and God entered my world on a fairly equal basis with hobgoblins and banshees. Even at seven, I rather doubted that God existed and was afraid he would punish me for thinking so. I feared there was evil in me to believe more in ghosts than I did in Him. I played upstairs very happily during the day, when I didn't believe that assorted horrors filled the attics, but I was terrified of being up there at night, when I did believe. I was especially afraid

146

of Mr. Rust. I'd seen him in a TV show, his evil face appearing in the metal of swing sets and aluminum siding, and I imagined that one night in my bedroom I'd look at the wall, and there he'd be, staring razorblades at me. The idea of that gaze frightened me more than anything he might do, because, though I felt that Mr. Rust would be confined by the wall, the palpable evil in his eyes would not be. My bed was pushed close to one wall, so I never ever slept on my right side, since if Mr. Rust did appear, I would be nose to nose with him and wouldn't stand a chance. If he appeared on the other wall, at least there would be some distance, some chance to escape his stare. In bed, as I huddled beneath the blankets, I imagined, though never heard, dry, shuffling sounds coming down the hall. If anything out there got me, it got me. I just didn't want to see it coming.

Although I tried to keep my fears secret, my parents sensed my terror of the upstairs, and sometimes Dad would tease me about it, as if trying to jolly me into the proper perspective. One fall night, after supper, when we were still sitting around the table, I realized I'd left a toy upstairs. I wanted it, but I didn't want to go up to get it. I held this tension inside me for a while and then decided to try a risky solution. I asked Nora if she would go upstairs and get it. Dad whooped: "He's too scared to go up himself, so he wants his baby sister to do it." Nora was probably four or five at the time, and I wanted to point out that she was no longer a baby, but I figured that would not do me any credit, and I squirmed in shame under my father's laughter. Yes, I had been perfectly willing to let my baby sister buy the farm on this mission. To me, she was expendable. Whatever it was that I wanted—I can't remember—I would have gladly left it upstairs. But now, the only alternative consistent with honor was to get it myself.

The door that opened to the stairs was next to the entrance to the kitchen. A full-length mirror was fastened to the door, and I contemplated myself for a while. Then I cautiously turned the handle, an oversized piece of glass, cut like a faceted diamond. It jiggled when I touched it, threatening to fall out of its socket. I opened the door, walked in, and flicked the light switch at the bottom of the stairs, fixing my eyes on the carpet as I started up. I didn't look up until I was about halfway to the top. That's when I came face to face with the angel.

I knew what angels looked like from Sunday school. They were invariably more male than female, blond, and blue-eyed. They helped kids across the street. They laid their invisible and unfelt arms on your shoulders, protecting you from the traffic, like adult safety patrolmen. If an angel had appeared by your side, you would have been startled for a second, but not frightened. Angels were like wise, powerful adults, but more reliable and friendly in their long white robes. The angel at the top of the stairs was nothing like this.

He, she, blocked the stairway, head scraping the ceiling, a figure sculpted out of light. Maybe if someone carved an angel out of ice, with the wings, and the gown, and shined a floodlight through it, into your eyes, so you could barely see, the light pouring into you like a barrage of cold needles, then the sight would be similar, but inadequate, because it wouldn't capture the fear. For the angel did not smile. It did not even immediately look at me, and if it had a message, it was wholly contained in the mere ferocity of its presence. My eyes and the angel's caught, as if locked to each other on an invisible line, from which I hung, gulping like a fish.

I struggled to break the gaze and finally snapped it. I bolted for the bottom of the stairs, slamming through the door and into the kitchen. Mom and Dad, still at the dinner table, looked at me in astonishment. Then Dad began to laugh, louder and louder, and I ran.

I never mentioned the angel to anyone.

I was confirmed in the Lutheran Church, Missouri Synod, and went with my parents to church every Sunday until I was eighteen, because they insisted. Going to church was like being held under water without reprieve, a baptism of boredom. Every week Pastor Schillenbeck's sermon dwelt on the turgid and swamplike character of the human heart and how thankful we should be that God allowed his only son to be slaughtered, slowly, for our benefit. I was a poor miserable sinner, justly deserving God's temporal and eternal punishment, but He'd come through for me for reasons unknown, and the only appropriate response was to spend as much time as possible groveling in thankfulness. When I went to college in 1970, I started reading Alan Watts and became very interested in eastern philosophy, where there was no personal god who bore grudges or demanded love from beings who had so egregiously let him down.

I did think about the angel occasionally. I tried to believe the power of my imagination had made me see what did not exist, but I could never buy that explanation completely. I wasn't the type to see things. When a hypnotist had come to town and performed at the high school, I was quickly let go as a volunteer for hypnosis. I wasn't suggestible enough. Maybe the angel was partly the reason I entered the world as one of those unmoored persons, so common in the last thirty years, who can't accept religion and can't make sense of the world without it. I thought life ought to have "meaning," but could find none, and went through Marx, existentialism, Jung, Erich Fromm, Joseph Campbell, and Zen, looking for it. Every idea had clay feet. Someone like Victor Frankel would come along, and I'd read him with hope that lasted, maybe, for a couple of days.

Deciding on a profession was no easier than picking an ideology. When I went to college, I tried geology, my father's idea, and argued with him for three years about not wanting to be a geologist. I had inherited some of Dad's enthusiasm for natural theology—but this didn't mesh, so far as I could see, with working for an oil company. Then I tried English literature as an alternative scripture. When there seemed to be no future in English, I went to law school, and after five years of trying to take lawsuits seriously, in 1982, I decided to go back to English and graduate school, where it did not take long to discover that postmodernism had dissolved even Matthew Arnold's last source of spiritual refuge. I was thirty, my daughter was six months old, my wife, Ruth, was trying to deal with leaving the suburbs for student housing, and my father was dying of lung cancer.

At first my dad thought his blood pressure medicine was just slowing him down. "I have to hargh out when I go up the stairs," he said. Dad had grown up speaking Bayerisch, a German dialect, and English together, and sometimes he made up his own words just for the fun of it. I talked to my parents once a week, on the phone, and Dad had begun to sound distant, exhausted. When I told him I was going to quit law and go back to graduate school, I expected him to give me an elaborate argument about why it was irresponsible, if not just plain nuts. But all he said was, "OK, it's your life." I felt disconnected for the rest of the day. My father and I had thrashed out every career decision I'd ever made. Usually he was in opposition to whatever it was that I wanted to do, and now, he'd finally relinquished the drama of my future. Next Sunday, on the phone, he told me he'd bought a *Physician's Desk Reference* and had begun reading about the effect of beta-blockers on heart rate.

"Why don't you see a doctor, Dad?"

"What's the point? I've got to stay on the medicine for my blood pressure. I'll just have to learn to live with it."

"Maybe they could give you something else."

"Well, maybe."

"How do you know for sure it's the blood pressure medicine?"

"What else could it be?"

By Easter, Dad had not touched a cigarette in a week, a feat he hadn't been able to accomplish since he'd gotten hooked on tobacco in the Twentieth Air Force. He was a different man to be around that Easter Sunday, calmer, happier than I'd seen him in years. He had been in the habit of spending his after dinner hours smoking, drinking instant coffee, and raging about the state of the country as revealed by *U.S. News and World Report*. This had gotten worse—obsessive even—over the last years of his life. He seemed to think that if he railed against the path of his country frantically enough, in a kind of anguished prayer, the sheer spiritual effort would somehow do it good. But that Easter, he seemed to realize, from somewhere deep within, that he was on a ride and someone else was driving. He could relax.

A week later he was in Harbor Beach Community Hospital for pneumonia. A week after that he was moved to St. Luke's in Saginaw because he might have lung cancer. I saw him the day after exploratory surgery. His chest was heavily bandaged, and tubes sprouted from the thickest part of the dressing like malignant yellow vines. An IV was plugged into his arm, a Foley catheter was under the covers, and an oxygen tube burrowed into his nostrils. The room was always too hot for him, and he kept pushing down the covers until even the top of his pubic hair sometimes showed. I was surprised that my father, a modest man, was not uneasy about this. It gave me moments of acute embarrassment. He had ceased to think of his body as his own. He was fifty-nine.

When the oncologist entered, my mother and sister were sitting in ugly orange plastic chairs, and I was leaning against the wall. The doctor was young, younger than I, and it seemed odd to have somehow gotten older than doctors. We all exchanged a few pleasantries, then the doctor said, "Your biopsy was positive for cancer, Dr. Kramer, and you also have a great deal of lung damage from emphysema."

Dad's eyes flashed like black marbles. "Now I'm in the riggin's," he muttered.

The doctor gave us a moment to absorb and then went on. "You don't have very much lung capacity left, and the cancer is growing in the healthy parts of your lungs. It is a fast-growing variety of squamous cell cancer. There are three possible treatments: chemotherapy, radiation, and surgery, or a combination of these. Whether to use any of these methods is ultimately up to you, but there are problems, in your case, with using any. We might use radiation to try to shrink the cancer to a smaller size, and then remove it surgically, but so much of your lung capacity is gone that you probably wouldn't be able to survive on what you have left. Chemo leaves us with the same problem, and both chemo and radiation would leave you feeling very, very sick."

Dad squinted at the doctor: "What do you mean?"

"I'm sorry. There's nothing we can do to treat this cancer."

"How much time do I have left?"

"It's hard to say. Maybe six weeks. Maybe six months."

"What would you do?"

The doctor hesitated. "The important thing, Dr. Kramer, is what you want to do. But if it was me, I'd try to make my remaining time as comfortable and enjoyable as possible. Chemo or radiation will just get in the way of that. They may extend your time a little, or they may not. But they will make you feel pretty sick for the time you've got left."

We must have looked like four owls perched in a barn, eyes unshuttered in perpetual surprise.

"Do you have any questions? Is there anything you'd like to talk about?"

"Can I go home?"

"In a few days, after you heal up from the exploratory. Home would really be the best place for you—it's a lot easier to get some rest out of the hospital, in your own bed. And there are plenty of oxygen services. You'll need the oxygen. We'll help you with that." The doctor waited. Finally he said, "Are there any questions?"

We looked at each other. "No, Dr. Thompson," my mother smiled wildly, as if she wanted to give this young man a cookie and milk.

"Well, if you have any questions, or you'd like to talk, just ask a nurse. I'll be around until 5:00," he said, a bit doubtfully, as he backed out of the room.

"Cancer," Dad said, and gestured to the bandages and tubes coming out of his chest. "Cancer, and they have to put me through this. They knew I had cancer anyway. Why the hell did they have to put me through this?"

"I guess they had to make sure," I said, wondering why I felt this obligation to answer rhetorical questions.

His shallow breathing was getting noticeably faster. He looked at the ceiling, then at us. "You haven't had lunch yet. You must be getting hungry. Why don't you go down to the cafeteria. I feel worn out."

I felt bad about leaving him then, and at the same time, relieved. He clearly wanted some time alone. We took the elevator down to the cafeteria, my mother, Nora, and I, and filed through the line for Sunday lunch. Chicken à la king. A roll. Salad. Free coffee, courtesy of St. Luke's, to the relatives of patients. We sat down. The food gradually disappeared. We talked about getting Dad home. Would he need an ambulance from Saginaw to Harbor Beach? Probably. My mother kept talking about the facts of the last month, as if setting them out often enough would make the situation clear to her. How Dad had been getting more and more tired. How he had to stop three times for breath on the way up the stairs. How he thought it was a side effect of his high blood pressure medicine. How he had gone into Harbor Beach Community for pneumonia. How one of the nurses there, one of Dad's longtime patients, had looked so concerned one day when she'd heard him breathing. And as an afterthought, where, Mom wondered, would Dad's patients go now that he couldn't practice optometry?

We stayed with him until 5:00, off and on, off and on, at least one of us always in the small, hot room. Outside, slush fell from the sky. An emaciated house painter lay in the next bed, a man who had smoked too many cigarettes and inhaled too much lead. His family was by his bed, a wife and grown daughter, friends came and went.

At midafternoon I had to get out, get some fresh air. I wandered to the gift shop. Bibles, crosses, and cards of a religious bent filled the racks. St. Luke's was a Lutheran hospital. In 1982 the angel fad had not yet hit the market: sightings of angelic flights were not yet as common as those of Canadian geese. Seraphim, chubby and pink like amoretti, did not decorate book covers or occupy an ontological niche next to auras and crystal power. But angels were on my mind. I bought a cheap New Testament, smaller than my hand, and took it outside, where in sight of my father's room, there were some slushy wooden benches. Snow still fell. I didn't care whether the book got wet or my pants got soaked. I sat down and after trying in a couple wrong gospels, found the story of the angel, after Jesus' Resurrection, in Matthew 28: "And, behold, there was a great earthquake: for the angel of the Lord descended from heaven, and came and rolled back the stone from the door, and sat upon it. His countenance was like lightning, and his raiment white as snow: And for fear of him the keepers did shake, and became as dead men." And became as dead men. Snow drops blotted the paper, and I thought of the angel at the top of the stairs, waiting. I thought of him waiting for my father, and eventually, for me. Would it be better to meet that angel again or to disappear, Buddhist fashion, like a snowflake on the pavement, losing myself in the trees and grass and the interstellar reaches between molecules?

At the end of the day, I drove from Saginaw to Grand Rapids, to Ruth and my daughter, Lynn. An invisible line divides southern Michigan into west and east, and I crossed it just west of Portland. Here, the flat farmland, made for corn, sugar beets, navy beans, and wheat, spotted by decaying industrial towns, gave way to rolling glacial hills and woodland. Crops shared the land with woods on a more equal basis, and rivers and creeks flowed faster, down steeper grades. The land lay dark, but a green phosphorescence filled the woods in the gray twilight. Spring was coming. The winter wheat already cast its green mist over the black soil.

A couple days later I took the day off and drove back to Saginaw. Dad looked better, so much so that the doctor's prognosis seemed unreal.

"The nurses keep coming in and asking me if I want to talk about it," he said. "What do they expect me to say? I talked to the doctor again. Asked him if there was any chance radiation or chemotherapy would work. He said no. Just said there was absolutely nothing that would help. That's a hell of a thing to tell a person. I've been talking to your mother. I know there are places in Mexico where they give treatments that aren't available here yet. Maybe we should check them out."

I was surprised at his attitude. Part of me wanted to him accept this death and make his peace with the world, to avoid a bitter and useless struggle that would raise expectations only to have them crushed. "Dad, we'll do whatever you want us to. I'll do whatever I can to make sure things get done your way."

"Thanks," he said. Tears came to his eyes and he sighed. "Maybe I'll just go home and wait it out. I don't have much energy for anything else. Those damn cigarettes. I was a god-damned fool."

"No you weren't, Dad."

"I should have quit years ago. I remember when you kids used to complain in the backseat about the cigarette smoke making you sick. I couldn't even quit then."

"It's hard. There are things I can't seem to stop myself from doing. I spend too much money. My VISA bill is always cranked out of sight. There are guys at the firm who have to stay late there until 10:00 at night and come in on weekends—they can't stop. Mom can't stop cleaning the house. We're all hooked."

Then he had to use the bedpan. I had to help get him on and hold him there, for a long time, while his bowels moved with excruciating slowness. After that was over, the respiratory therapist came in, a pretty girl who Dad obviously liked. I went outside to the wet benches.

Mom felt the frozen anger she always felt when God had cheated on their agreement: "Why do these things always have to happen to me?" was her refrain. She had faithfully gone to church, Women's Missionary League, taught Sunday school, vacation Bible school, and done extra duty in the church basement for congregational dinners, pouring coffee by the gallon. She had done her best to raise her children as good Lutherans, dutifully forced my sister and me to memorize enough of the Bible and *Luther's Small Catechism* to get confirmed, and hauled me, under protest, to church. And now, as had happened many times in the past, trouble was coming into her life that she did not deserve, and yet, if she did not deserve it, why did she feel the weight of judgment upon her? "I haven't done anything wrong," she might have shrieked, at times, in the crowded hospital elevator, but that would have been followed by the doubt, and then the certainty, that she *must* have done something wrong, which made her all the more angry and all the more determined to deny her own guilt, whatever it might be. Her bewilderment showed itself in continual accounts of the last few weeks, as if she were trying to disbelieve them. Sometimes, in the middle of these narratives, she'd issue a pronouncement that after Dad was gone, maybe she'd buy a condo in Florida. "And what am I going to do with the house?" she looked at me in accusation. "I can't take care of it myself!"

On the day before Dad was set to go home, my aunt's second husband, Del Trinklein, came to visit him. Del was spare in the middle, of medium height with sandy gray hair. A retired building contractor, he looked years younger than someone who, by my mother's calculations, based on confirmations, baptisms, and graduations, must have been at least sixty-five. He'd married my aunt several years after Dad's older brother Tom had died; now he carpentered a bit, gardened, and spent hours on Bible study and prayer meetings of an un-Lutheranlike (at least for that time) charismatic bent. He was a sincere man, and I liked him, though his religious enthusiasm often made me cringe.

Dad was obviously glad to see him, and they talked about odds and ends for half an hour. Then Del took a deep breath, looked at the ceiling of the room, and seemed to inflate. He asked my father in a voice which had suddenly dropped half an octave, "Johnny, will you pray with me?"

Red rose around Dad's neck and ears. "Sure," he mumbled. He was too good to spurn real concern, and never would have denied the efficacy of prayer. But he had never been prayed *over*, and was not the type of man to relish it.

"Oh Lord, if it be thy will . . ." Del intoned.

Dad cast a glance in my direction, part plea, part mortification.
". . . please help Johnny to recover from his illness . . ."

Only people from Dad's childhood ever called him Johnny.

". . . and give him courage during this time of trial. Be a
strength to his family and those who love him . . ."

Dad resolutely looked at the lump his feet made under the covers.

". . . and if it be thy will that he not recover, help them to accept
it, and to understand that one day they will all meet again together. In Jesus name we ask it, Amen."

Del paused for a while, with his eyes closed, as if waiting for
an echo to that "Amen," which my father finally gave him.

Dad soon went home from St. Luke's. Ruth and Lynn and I
went to see him the weekend after. He was seated in a La-Z-Boy
rocker, which we covered with a fleece rug, so he wouldn't get
bedsores. His feet were thick and puffy, and he had the footrest
up as high as it would go. Next to him there was an oxygen tank
from which a tube led to his nose. His face was becoming skull-
like, and purple flesh hung like tea bags under his eyes.

"I have horrible dreams," he said, matter-of-factly, "but I can't
sleep. I can't lay down in bed because I can't get enough air. So I
stay up all night, in the chair, or at the kitchen table. I don't sleep,
but I dream anyway."

"What are your dreams like?" I asked.

"Horrible, horrible."

He talked about politics. The hostages in Iran. He laughed. We
watched a Jock Mahoney Tarzan movie. "We'll meet each other
again someday. After we die," Dad said. He knew I didn't believe it.

Another week dragged toward another Sunday. Mom bought
a new Ford Mercury. Dad spent hours with his accountant and
his stockbroker, getting everything set just right. He sold his optometry practice to two young men fresh out of Ferris State. I
drew up the contract. I rewrote Mom's and Dad's wills and got a
local lawyer to handle Dad's probate. Dad was having a lot of

trouble getting air and went back to Harbor Beach Community. Meanwhile, work was piling up on my desk in Grand Rapids. I wasn't sleeping. It was mid-May.

Tuesday night I went to bed early and had a dream. I was driving a crowded little foreign car. My mother, my wife, my sister, and I were packed in. Dad sat gray and rigid in the back with Mom and Nora. Stubble stood out on his hollowed face and his black, exhausted eyes stared straight ahead, intelligent but cold. We were lost, but unconcerned about it, checking the map, driving in a land of canyons, peaks, and brilliant early morning sunshine, which wedged its way through billowing black clouds. We drove an immaculate road—no signs, no wires, no fence. We came to a village of gothic buildings and Tudor houses. By this time the sky had become a shifting mass of cobalt. Lightning flashed, but there was no thunder. Finally, we found what we were looking for. It was a cafe with many outdoor tables. A little bed of coals in a brazier burned in the middle of each table. We took Dad out of the car and sat him stiffly in a wicker chair. Orange light from the coals flickered on one side of his face. This is where we'd be able to find him. A few drops of rain fell. Dad made no move, spoke no word. Mom, Nora, and Ruth had disappeared. I got back in the car, drove off, and awoke to find the sun on my sheets and Ruth breathing lightly beside me. A cardinal sang.

I went to work, and at 4:00 my mother called. The doctor didn't think Dad would last the night. I took this as a fact. I got home as fast as I could, told Lynn what was happening, and hit the road. I drove my aging Accord at eighty miles per hour until I passed Lansing. I thought that I might never be with my father again, and he would know I hadn't been there. That maybe right now he was longing to see me, and the only way I could tell him how much I loved him, to ever make him know that, was to be holding his hand right now. That he might already be dead. After Lansing I sometimes hit ninety.

As I passed Frankenmuth and drove east toward Richville, the sun was setting, and a thunderstorm looked to be starting in the northeast. The woodlots were nearly in full leaf, and the sun drove golden shafts through the trees. The leaves vibrated with it. The white steeple of the Lutheran church in Richville glowed against the thunderheads behind it. I pulled up to the town's only intersection, just after a big brown Buick Riviera, a B-52 of an automobile, scuffed and dirty, came up on my left. It was the kind of car a high school kid with criminal tendencies would buy, fix, and then try to smash, and I immediately assumed the driver was male, though I wasn't paying attention. He beat me to the intersection, but I coasted through the stop sign ahead of him. His crate looked like it could barely move, and I didn't want to get stuck behind it on a two-lane road. But as soon as we got out of town, he tailgated me, doing seventy, for three miles, and then with a roar, pulled around me and tore off.

I slowed down, shaken. A few miles down the road I caught up with him. He was going about ten miles an hour. The small rear window was filthy, and I couldn't see through. I moved into the oncoming traffic lane to pass him, and he swerved left. I hit the brakes and swerved back, missing him by a foot. "Damn it!" I roared. Both cars now sat motionless on the highway. My heart started to pound. He started up, and I followed. We were back in the right lane, going ten miles an hour. I tried to pass him again. He swerved again, nearly sending me into the deep ditch on the opposite side of the road. My teeth were clamped so tight my jaw muscles began to hurt. I wanted to keep calm. To detach myself. I was in a situation I would just have to wait out. As I crept along at ten miles an hour, I found myself wishing I had a gun. I visualized sticking it out the window and blowing out his rear windshield, and then perhaps, blowing out the rear of his head.

I could take a side road, go three miles out of my way on gravel, and get back on M-141, but there was no guarantee that the son-of-a-bitch wouldn't follow me. His car was faster and way heavier than mine. I didn't want to try to pass him again. I thought if I could only talk to him, "My father is dying, let me through," that any halfway decent human being, even this idiot, would understand. I pictured him as a skinny eighteen-year-old kid with acne, long hair, and a pack of cigarettes rolled up in his T-shirt sleeve, and as my hands bulged on the steering wheel I longed to get them around his throat.

We crept along at ten miles an hour, then his brake lights came on, and I slammed my car to a stop inches from his back fender. He pulled ahead a few yards. I followed and he hit his brakes again. In one motion I put the car in neutral, cranked back the parking brake, released my seat belt and was out the door with my eye on the driver's side of the Buick. The number or size of the occupants never entered my head. I grabbed at the driver's door and saw a greasy shock of long blonde hair. He turned to me, and all I can remember are his eyes, cerulean blue, so blue I imagined, for an instant, that deep in his skull they must be connected by an electric arc. I heard the squeal of tires. Blue smoke rose from the road as the car drifted toward me, trying to grab the asphalt, until the wheels caught, jerked, howled, and the Buick launched itself east. I stood in the middle of the road and screamed into his exhaust. Then I went back to my car and drove very slowly toward Caro. I waited for the Buick to reappear, but it didn't.

By the time I got to Cass City the sky was black. The thunderheads in the north and east had clotted and heat lightning was playing around the edges of the clouds, illuminating the great billowing heaps. I pushed to ten miles over the speed limit and felt calmer. Branches lashed in the wind. I overdrove the entrance to Harbor Beach Community, wheeled around, and cut into the parking lot. It was 9:30. I got Dad's room number from the receptionist and took the stairs, two and three at a time, to the second floor.

Mom and Dad's sister, Laura, were outside the room, standing in the door, as if they wanted to go in but were simply too frightened.

"What's happening?" I said.

My mother was wilted, gray. "He hasn't said anything since 6:00. Go in. Maybe he'll talk to you."

Dad lay on his back. No sheet covered him, and big, fluorescent ceiling lights, every light in the room, were on. His eyes were three-quarters shut, as if he were meditating. The nurses had put a diaper contraption on him. It was all he was wearing. The ceiling lights left no shadow. Didn't they think the light might hurt his eyes? That it would be better to die among shadows, with the covers pulled up to his chin, to hide his naked and unstrung body? I looked for a light switch and didn't see one.

His breaths came far apart, gulps of air without rhythm. I took his hand. It was hot and dry. "Dad. It's me. I'm here. Can you hear me?" I said, very softly. He took a deep breath. It sounded as if he were gargling molasses and gravel. Then he relaxed, his eyes closed, and he exhaled long and deeply, as if expelling his soul. He'd waited for me, and then he'd let go; I was sure of that.

The nurse ushered my mother, aunt, and me into a little room with a cross. The minister from Our Savior Lutheran joined us and said a prayer. The nurse asked us whether we wanted some coffee. I said yes. We stared at the pot, sitting on a table between us. When we got outside the hospital, the wind was blowing. A drop or two of slanting rain hit me in the face. I looked up, and a stroke of lightning lit the clouds, blue and rough, like the underside of an unshaven face.

That night I went home with my mother to the house my parents had built and moved to many years after I saw the angel. We sat for a while, in the kitchen, and then went to bed. My mother and aunt were in the downstairs bedrooms, leaving me the upstairs. There was no door to this staircase, which was utterly open and innocuous. There were no attics up there. No Mr. Rust. I went up a couple steps, paused for a long time, and then walked down. I got a blanket from the linen closet and spent the night on the living room couch.

Do you have a box holding odds and ends from old games? Perhaps inside, there is a fifty-one–card deck. (Or maybe just an ace of spades.) A few odd Monopoly pieces, perhaps a pawn or two from a chess set that has otherwise disappeared. A checker. A die. I have a mental box like that. It contains an angel, an outlaw Buick, and the way a spring day can open up as if it had four dimensions instead of three. It has bits and pieces of experience that don't fit into the world my teachers in geology, law, and literature mapped out, scraps that changed me slowly, because though I tried, I couldn't deny they were there, in the box, rattling around.

Did you know it is possible, though stupendously improbable, that all of the gas molecules in your general vicinity could, in an instant, take up residence elsewhere, leaving you gasping in a vacuum? (Perhaps they are heading toward a corner of the room right now.) Or that some subatomic particles seem to move backward in time? That others act as if they knew the future or could read minds? That some physical systems are so complex and chaotic it is impossible, even at a macroscopic level, to predict how they will change or what they will do? Which is to say, contra Hume, that even our physics leaves room for the miraculous. In such a universe, couldn't angels exist? Would a resurrection really be so hard to pull off? At some point does it stretch credulity further to believe in a world which is purely and solely material than one which is not?

I am only a decade short of fifty-nine. I have become a Roman Catholic, and although this once would have appalled my father, I assume that now, he would understand. The Church year is regular, but full of change, and there are miracles every day. The priest breaks the bread. The monstrance passes by. Babies are baptized. At Mass, sometimes I imagine the dead, all about me. They are jammed in the pews, the aisles, everywhere, worshipping with the rest of us. "I believe in *all* things seen and unseen," we say, not knowing what we mean. Yet it has become unreasonable for me to believe in anything less.

ABOUT THE AUTHOR

Craig Bernthal is Professor of English at California State University in Fresno. He is the author of *The Trial of Man: Christianity and Judgment in the World of Shakespeare.*